The Derelict Light

A NOVEL

MIKE STARK

University of Nebraska Press • Lincoln

The University of Nebraska Press is part of a land-grant institution
with campuses and programs on the past, present, and future
homelands of the Pawnee, Ponca, Otoe-Missouria, Omaha, Dakota,
Lakota, Kaw, Cheyenne, and Arapaho Peoples, as well as those
of the relocated Ho-Chunk, Sac and Fox, and Iowa peoples.

Library of Congress Cataloging-in-Publication Data
Names: Stark, Mike (Journalist), author.
Title: The derelict light: a novel / Mike Stark.
Description: Lincoln: University of Nebraska Press, [2023]
Identifiers: LCCN 2022056839
ISBN 9781496235220 (paperback)
ISBN 9781496237217 (epub)
ISBN 9781496237224 (pdf)
Subjects: LCSH: Fires—Oregon—Astoria—History—20th
century—Fiction. | BISAC: FICTION / Literary | FICTION /
Historical / General | LCGFT: Historical fiction. | Novels.
Classification: LCC PS3619.T37368 D47 2023 |
DDC 813/.6—dc23/eng/20230403
LC record available at https://lccn.loc.gov/2022056839

Set in Whitman by K. Andresen.
Designed by L. Welch.

The Derelict Light

Prologue

December 8, 1922

Smoke and the last of the flames were still raking downtown when the kid found the lumberjack hanging from Sanborn's dock. One end of the rope was triple-wrapped around a Douglas fir plank, the other knotted around his neck, cinched up to his chin in a way that forced his stubbled jaw off to one side. He had wet himself, and one of his eyelids hung half-open like an unfinished thought.

Just a few minutes before, the boy had watched as looters rifled through what was left of the ticket office at the Blue Mouse Theatre, stuffing money and movie tickets into their coat pockets before scurrying toward the bank, chasing rumors that one of the safes had split open in the searing heat. The front window at Owl Drug was blown out, so the boy grabbed a lemon drop from the display before hustling down Commercial Street and then Eighth to get to the river and out of the bitter smoke. The man's body was dangling below a rust-colored warehouse, the tips of his cracked black shoes hovering just above the slick rocks at the water's edge. An inch or two taller and he could've stood up and maybe pulled himself free of his predicament. No matter now.

The boy had seen dead bodies before. Just a few weeks earlier he'd been fishing from the jetty when some men dragged Paavo Kastell out of the Columbia's mouth, his gray lips nearly smiling as if he'd been relieved not to face another season with hardly any salmon in the river. This stranger on the rope wore exhaustion all over his face and body. The boy lingered just long enough to tug on the leg of the man's pants. Satisfied he was dead, the boy clambered up the big rocks and disappeared into the smoke for another look at hell having its way with Astoria, Oregon.

Part 1 *Ruin*

Chapter 1

1879

Arni Leino never meant to find himself in Astoria. His father, Joseph, had arrived first, abandoning fields of failing wheat in his native Finland for the far west of America to see if the stories were true: that the Columbia River was so full of riches that each salmon came with a dollar in its mouth and never asked for change.

Leaving behind his wife and two children, Joseph set off with his good friend Jorma Olli and took an ocean trip so long and stomach-churning they thought it might never end. After crossing the Atlantic and then around devilish Cape Horn and heading north in the Pacific, the two finally arrived in Astoria in the spring of 1879 with a suitcase between them and barely enough money to share a meal. They went down to the cannery docks the first morning and talked their way onto a fishing crew. The men they replaced had failed to show up after a fierce night of drinking and the crew chief, a thick-necked Irishman, sized them up in the gray rain, barely caring they could only speak a few words of English.

"No one'll be discussing modern events," he'd said with a shrug, motioning them down a long wooden walkway.

Hundreds of small, pitching boats were already on the river, like water bugs flitting along the surface of a pond. Joseph and Jorma were put in a twenty-four-foot wooden boat with a white canvas sail that looked like half a wing incapable of flight, much less of pulling this double-ended tub across the Columbia, whose distant shore seemed miles away. A third man on the boat—they never learned his name, a colorless figure all soft edges and mist—directed Jorma toward the oars and Joseph toward the nets in the boat's belly while he manned the sail and pushed off the dock with one foot. There wasn't time for Joseph to do anything more than

5

swallow his terror of the open water. With the sail down, the current pulled them west toward the mouth and the Pacific beyond, calmly at first and then faster as the river narrowed and became shallower over a vast bed of shifting sand beneath a sheet of swirling water. Joseph held his breath as the boat chattered over tiny sharp waves that grew into big, rounded swells whose troughs eventually became so deep he sometimes lost sight of the horizon.

Joseph and Jorma said nothing as their captain steered them wordlessly into the river's maw, sending a steady wash of bitter cold water—salty, but not as salty as the ocean itself—across their faces. Finally the captain gave the signal for the net to be tossed over the side. Jorma fed it over the gunwales, gingerly at first, but the captain grew impatient. He said something in a language Jorma couldn't understand, but the message was conveyed and Jorma, ignoring the pain in his hands from the net's brittle edges, began dumping it over the side in double time.

There were three nets in all, each with floats at the top and a weighted line along the bottom. Once the nets were out, Joseph and Jorma silently sat back on their haunches, following the lead of their captain, as the boat rose and fell on the waves. Joseph finally had a chance to take in the captain's face and found he was young, perhaps not yet twenty, judging by the feather of a blond mustache beneath his nose. The young leader's mood had brightened by now with the nets in the water. While they waited he motioned with his hands about how the nets worked: hanging in the water like curtains with square openings wide enough for a fish to swim into but then be caught by their gills, trapped until the nets were pulled back into the boats.

"Chinook," he said, making a swimming-fish motion with his hand.

"Chinook," the two newcomers repeated in unison.

"Very good money for Chinook," the captain said. "The best salmon on the Columbia."

An hour later, as the tide started to change, they hauled in the nets, and the Finns marveled at the bounty of stunned silvery fish that were attached and floundering in their grasp. They again followed the captain's lead in plucking them from the net and tossing them into the center of the boat. Soon they put the sails up, employed the oars, and rode the incoming current back toward Astoria, the bottom of the boat lined with piles of wide-eyed fish, some still working their jaws in desperation. Joseph and Jorma smiled at each other as they neared the shore.

"We'll eat tonight," Joseph told his friend.

"And maybe tomorrow too!" came the reply.

After the first week, they were given their own boat to use, with Jorma handling the tiller in the stern and Joseph on the bow with the nets. They followed the other men in boats, careful not to stray too far but mindful not to set their nets too close to anyone else's. That's how fights started, and there was no time for fighting in a place like this.

The roiling collision between the Columbia and the Pacific, Joseph and Jorma would learn from the others, was a pitiless place that swallowed ships and souls with equal appetite. The river bottom was littered with hundreds of wrecks and the bones of many more men—some hapless, some overly confident, and many who were perfectly capable in nearly all circumstances at sea but were still swept into the ocean's vastness and made unseen by the world forever after.

"If there's a place where the devil is happier," a fisherman with missing front teeth had told Joseph by way of a toast at the end of a long, terrible, rain-swept day on the river, "I'd hate to see it."

Joseph and Jorma fished all spring and summer, hauling in giant Chinooks, reds, and steelheads. The water was a battlefield where desperate men did whatever it took to gain advantage over one another: slicing ropes, colliding with other boats to drive them from a fruitful ribbon of fish, swamping, lying, shouting, even shooting if it came to that. Any beef that wasn't resolved on the river was finished on the docks, where bloodstains somehow found a way to outlast the rain. On the river, though, the men gathered salmon like one gathers breath after nearly suffocating. The fish, plucked from nets and even snatched from the water by the quickest of hands, were the currency of survival. Those who had it lived and ate, drank and danced till past late on Saturday nights. Those who didn't, well, who was to say? Hume's cannery paid four cents per pound—half that at first, until Joseph and Jorma compared prices with some of the other fishermen, learned they were getting short-changed, and demanded equal pay one afternoon in a half-drunken visit to the cannery offices perched high on the docks above the Columbia. Some of the money went back to their families in Finland; the rest went to the saloon and the landlord of the perpetually cold room they rented above Sire's Hardware.

When they went back to Finland for the winter, Jorma met a woman, a giant, loving creature who resembled a bear. He didn't want to return to Astoria.

"You'll have a family soon enough," Joseph had countered. "You'll need something to build your nest with."

"The only nest I need is the one in her bed." Jorma smiled.

Arni Leino and his sister, Lily, begged their father not to return to America. The spring and summer had been too hard without him as they tended to their small collection of sheep and tried to keep the wheat fields viable. Joseph shook his head. "We'll remain poor forever if I stay." Joseph wore down his friend, too, over a series of fires in his hearth and too many glasses of *sima*, the fermented mead left over from the warmer months. They were back in Astoria the next April, just as the spring freshets, energized by snow melting from faraway mountains, pulsed down the Columbia like a runaway train. More canneries had been built over the winter and the mood—at least among those in the boats—was thick with optimism. Jorma and Joseph picked up where they left off, soon enough riding a slack tide in a two-sailed butterfly boat rented from the cannery men at Hume's.

The fishing was good for several weeks and then a sudden warm spell disgorged even more melted mountain snow into the Columbia, filling the muddy sloughs and topping the banks between Clatskanie and the mouth. A vicious storm followed one morning in early May, just as the fishermen were flirting with the edge of the bar and laying out their nets. Within minutes, the seas were roiling, first with breakers ten feet high, then twenty, and soon forty. Giant walls of blue-gray water were decorated with lacy webs of white, swirling foam. Jorma and Joseph, caught in the morning fury, exchanged looks with the men in a nearby boat, who were wide-eyed and momentarily frozen in fear. Soon the nets behind them dragged against the waves, allowing deep flushes of water to flood over the gunwales. At one point their boat collided with the other in a clamorous valley of water, and Jorma saw their crew furiously sawing away their nets with huge knives.

"Christ, cut the nets!" Jorma shouted to his partner.

As their boat slid to the top of a two-story wave and down the back side, Jorma and Joseph scrambled for the knives in their belts—cheap blades that they'd each been told to buy before entering the Columbia on their own. The rain and the sea washed over them as they huddled in the bow. Jorma was the first to free his knife and began ripping desperately at the nets. Joseph fumbled with his wet hands, unable to undo the blade from his belt, and instead gripped the gunwales and braced himself against the violence toying with their vessel. Finally the first net broke free and was yanked into the river, taking Jorma's knife with it. Jorma cursed and turned toward Joseph in exasperation. Just then, the weight in the boat shifted as it crested a wave. Joseph had only a split second to see his friend's stricken face before Jorma was snatched overboard—backward, headfirst, boots last—into a maw of roaring, raging turmoil that only rose and fell again and again with the kind of murderous indifference it always had.

For the next two weeks, Joseph Leino traveled each day out to Clatsop Spit, a remote beach on the south side of the river mouth where deep, frothy waves churned relentlessly. "When someone disappears into the river, sometimes the body finds its way to the spit," he was told, "but many times it is simply gone." Joseph spent hours waiting in the tall, wet grass near the water, watching for signs of his friend in the mesmerizing eddies. *Where do we go when we can't return home again?* He imagined his friend's body drifting from one current to the next, first along the coast and then out to the impossibly vast sea. *Was his face up toward the sun and the rain or facedown into the blue-black water that seemed to have no bottom?*

Too many had died that spring and summer of 1880. The salmon were running hard, and the prices had yet to take their inevitable tumble. With the glut, the fishermen had flooded the river. Some mornings there were 1,500 boats scattered across the Columbia's mouth. When the spring storms came, as they always did, death danced happily in the waves. Perhaps two hundred men perished that season, many in the same morning Jorma was stolen. *At least you'll not be lonely on your journey, ystava,* Joseph told his friend while he stood, arms folded, on Clatsop Spit. *Many join you in finding out what's on the other side.*

Joseph returned to Astoria with a hole in his chest and darkness hanging over his shoulders. It took him till the end of summer to write to Jorma's family. He enclosed all the money he had but couldn't tell the story of what had happened in the boat, only that there had been a terrible storm on the river and Jorma was dead. "I am sorry that I brought him here and sorry that I am unable to do anything more than this letter. He was a good man and should have never been on that boat with me." He couldn't bear to imagine the scene on the other side of the world when his fiancée and family opened the letter.

Joseph wrote a similar letter to his own family in Finland, explaining what happened to his friend and saying he would stay in Astoria for the rest of the fishing season and return home in the winter. *Is a lie a lie if it keeps some silly hope alive?*

Joseph didn't return to Finland, and his wife back home died of pneumonia the following autumn. Unsure whether their father lived or not, Arni and his younger sister Lily went to live with their Aunt Olava and Uncle Remi, spending their early years in a confused fog, working on the family's farm and attending school down the road. They wrote to their father many times a year at the only address they had—the place he and Jorma had shared—and never got a response.

"He's dead. I can feel it in my heart," Lily said one day as they walked home from school.

It wasn't like her to take such a grim view. Arni was quiet and sometimes dour, but Lily had a lightness that always found its way out through her blue eyes, even on those dark, frigid days that left their countrymen wondering if it might be warmer in a grave underground. Lily laughed often, which usually made her brother laugh.

Nevertheless Remi and Olava saved money to pay for Arni and Lily to go to Astoria. He was twenty-two and she was nineteen. They made the passage on a ponderous ship called the *Peggy Ellis*, which took four months to get from Inkoo to San Francisco along much the same route their father had taken. From there, a lumber supply ship took them up the coast to Astoria. They'd never seen so many trees as they did on the bluffs just beyond the beach—what little daylight arrived at the trunks in front died before it could reach the third tree back.

They found their father working in a noisy salmon cannery alongside a chattering group of Chinese men and women. He was gray and sullen and barely seemed surprised when they tugged on his coat as he left the docks at the end of his shift. He pursed his lips with the news of his wife's death years before and kept walking toward the steep hills on the south edge of downtown. *Jorma*, he sighed to himself, *and now Alice.*

Lily wept at seeing her father for the first time in so many years, then cried twice as hard relaying the news of their mother, then harder still as their father recounted Jorma's story in a slow, hollow voice. They walked along the edge of the river aimlessly as each piece of news was told and questions were answered.

"Let us take you home, Papa," Lily said, stopping their walk. "There's nothing for you here but fish and bad memories."

He shrugged. "And back home, what waits?"

They stayed in Joseph's tiny basement room in a boarding house behind a market. Joseph forbade Arni from working on a fishing boat, so he found a job on the docks, unloading cargo ships and making repairs to the pier. His father stayed at the cannery and barely spoke when they gathered each night for dinner at the wooden table Arni had fashioned from stolen planks. Joseph gave his daughter the hay mattress he'd been sleeping on, and he and Arni slept on the floor beneath a giant wool blanket. Lily, always closer to her father than her mother, withdrew too, and everyone seemed satisfied to let the dense marine air fill the room rather than idle words.

Joseph was out of work the next winter with the canneries shut down. He grew ill and died quickly, overtaken by a dry cough that evolved into a heaving monster that seemed determined to expel every drop of fluid in his lungs. He was tired at the end. There was no peace, but Arni detected a grudging sense of relief on the last rainy night when the coughs finally subsided from lack of energy. "Pneumonia," the landlord said when he stopped by during Joseph's last hours. "The old man's best friend. Accept the blessing."

A month or so later, when the first tulip sprouts appeared, Arni stopped stirring his morning coffee and turned to Lily. "I'm going home. Come with me. Our homeland, our beloved *Suomi*, is still holding a life for us."

By then, though, Lily had made new friends: a group of young women who smoked cigarettes and ate at restaurants and sometimes played cards together, though no one mentioned where the money came from. On the doorstep of a new century, Astoria was a city on the cusp of something. The streets buzzed with the kind of frenetic energy borne by people busily propelling themselves toward an uncertain future. She worked as a waitress at the Port House, making enough to cover the basics, and ran with a ravenous young crowd that lit up the city nights with hollers and screams. Arni was less social and had fallen into a hole, wondering what had become of his father and his mother and Jorma and the endless stream of people he'd known in his short years who had fallen out of this world and into the next.

Lily patted her brother on the shoulder and fixed on his eyes. "Do what you want. I'm staying."

Chapter 2

1922

Two mornings after the fire, H. H. Flemming boarded a train in downtown Portland bound for Astoria, which was far west along the coast. Dreary as it was, Oregon's winter light hurt her eyes. It felt like a cold slab of steel slowly screwing its way through the back half of her skull. Before she left, her sister, Rachel, had done her best to fix her up, but her home remedies never did much good against the rot she drank.

"An inferior challenger against a superior enemy," Flemming told Rachel as she gathered her bag and notebooks for the trip. "What is that, goat's milk or something? My head feels like it weighs fifty pounds."

"You should be used to the weight by now," Rachel said. "You swallowed enough last night to give the Willamette a run for its money."

"Oh please," Flemming said, swiping down the wrinkles of her wool pants before pulling on a thick coat. "It was more than that."

The train helped. Between naps, she went through the morning and afternoon newspapers, reading everything she could about the fire. Most of the town was apparently gone: the banks, two department stores, the fancy new Weinhard Hotel, flimsy boarding houses, the entire downtown business district. She made mental notes about the three or maybe four people dead: a heart attack, a drowning, and a hanging. Someone else missing but maybe not dead. An ear that had been torn off in the chaos. No one died in the flames themselves, so there was that small mercy.

Flemming knew Astoria well enough. She'd been there for arsons, insurance scams, revenge fires and a string of kerosene jobs pulled by the radicals and labor agitators on shops deemed unfriendly to the local workers. There were industrial explosions, coal piles accidentally ignited, and the regular visitation that fire paid upon cheaply made and carelessly heated wooden houses and buildings, which were most of them. She checked them off in her head. Wilson Brothers' dry cleaning had been a total loss. The shoe-shine operation downtown had been set aflame by the owner's brother in a fit of rage over a woman they didn't know they were sharing. There were other fires at the Columbia Packing Company and the Oregon Café—probably for insurance money. Just a couple months earlier, the Hammond Mill on the port's west end had been swallowed whole by flames in a matter of minutes, stealing the jobs of nine hundred men. Flemming fell half-asleep thinking maybe that had been an accident but knew it probably wasn't.

The train made its way through Scappoose and St. Helens on a slow, twisting route where the Columbia River came and went from view. The train then settled into the long, dark stretch of forest near Rainier. Outside the windows was an endless green wall of trees and ferns and God knows what else. It wasn't until long after Clatskanie that Flemming caught the first whiff of salty coastal air, something between decay and rejuvenation.

Flemming liked coming to Astoria. *Always plenty to drink and always a whiff or two of trouble.* Portland had turned a corner, she'd noticed, and decided it needed to become more cosmopolitan, more European, more a city that bothered to disguise its stench with perfume. Astoria was no such place. That was her sense. Yes, the city was sick and knew it and mostly liked it that way, stubbornly dug in at the edge of the continent where the rain hardly ever seemed to stop falling, stewing in its own juices. There were vice and crime aplenty, but there was ambition too—to be the West Coast's most bustling port, the world's salmon supplier, and the hub for the endless source of logs in the forest outside town. *We are close,* the town leaders would say with each new dreamed-up scheme before its inevitable collapse. *We are very close.* Flemming liked that about Astoria in the same way she thought it'd be captivating to watch a snake eat its own tail.

The train finally stopped on the banks of the Columbia just a few blocks from downtown. No one greeted Flemming and she was glad of it. Her head still hurt, and she wanted to take a look around without any yammering in her ear. She rose from her seat, pulled on her coat and hat, and surveyed the town through the train windows.

"Good lord," she muttered.

The papers had printed photos and vivid descriptions of the fire, but they did it no justice. This was a wartime landscape of leveled buildings, collapsed streets, and shell-shocked citizens in soot-smeared coats wandering helplessly from block to block. *The sprinkling of pretty white snow on top of it all is a nice touch*, Flemming thought as she stepped off the train. *Sort of like handing a condemned man flowers on his way to the hangman's tower.*

Flemming liked that she didn't have to wear a uniform. It allowed her to move about without getting hassled by people looking for help. She drew enough attention as it was; she was as tall as most men, a little burly too, and had long since tired of the snide comments that her parents must've been hemlocks or maples or spruces. Her father had taught her not to allow an insult to go unanswered. "Verbal if you can, physical if you must," he'd said, and he instructed her in the art of both.

She picked her way through town but had to use her memory to know what street she was on and what had been there before. Over there was the only remaining wall of the marine supply store, and over there were the buckled ruins of the Weinhard Hotel; the two ionic columns that once served as its grand entrance were now stranded and alone, naked in the wispy light.

There was a crowd at the YMCA, a squat brick building just outside the fire's edge, right where the city's sandy river flats met the steep hill above town. Clusters of men were standing around outside sipping coffee, talking idly, and looking unsure about what to do next. Inside there were tables with pots of stew, bread, and coffee on a stove. One of the cooks—a smiling gray-haired woman who ran the hotel where she'd stayed after the Hammond Mill fire back in October—recognized Flemming.

"Inspector," she said, wiping her hands on a towel. "Just couldn't stay away, huh?"

"Hard to when the city keeps putting out the welcome mat like this. Can't say that you all don't keep me in business." She stared out one of the windows facing the city. "To be honest, I've never seen anything like it."

"Nor us. We've fed north of five hundred people out of here just in the last little while. No one's panicked yet, but any store left standing is seeing their shelves empty faster than they can get resupplied."

"And your hotel?" she asked, reaching into her memory for the woman's name but failing to find it.

The woman shook her head and tried to laugh. "Nah. We thought it'd be fine. It was plenty far from where the fire started, but it moved fast. Before we knew it, it was at our doorstep and then barging in like a squall. We managed to save the furniture in the lobby, but that was it. Everything else is just . . . gone." She lifted her chin in challenge against the pain.

"I'm really sorry to hear that, Mrs. Mattis," Flemming said, hoping she'd remembered right. She jabbed a thumb over her shoulder at the groups of men grumbling together, their hands wrapped around coffee mugs. "These hens lifting a finger?"

Mrs. Mattis cocked an eyebrow. "What do you think?"

"I think that's what I thought. Have you heard anything about how it started?"

"Leb says he's got it all figured." Mrs. Mattis pointed to a smaller room off to one side. "See for yourself."

Flemming showed herself in to see Leb Karlsson, the chief of police, who was talking to a man in uniform. She liked Karlsson, a man who did his best to keep some semblance of order in the city but had his own degenerate heart. Most bootleggers tended to get a free pass from him, provided he got his own cut. Flemming knew as much from her visits to Astoria and was well aware that public opinion of the city's top lawman depended on where one fell on prohibition. The high moralists and teetotalers—those who abstained from alcohol—regarded him as an enabler of sin and violence and degradation. The rest saw him as someone who allowed, within reason, the city to do what came naturally, rough edges and all, so long as it didn't get out of hand.

The chief looked genuinely happy to see Flemming in the doorway and invited her in to meet the other man in the room, a grim-faced lieutenant from the army station near Fort Vancouver.

"Hell of a thing," Flemming said. "How'd it start?"

"Basement of Thiel's," the chief said, motioning back toward downtown where Thiel's Pool Hall once stood. "It seemed clear to most everyone that's where it started, and it just blew up from there. Reeks pretty good of kerosene, so there isn't much doubt."

"So troublemakers . . . or is someone too far behind on their books?"

Karlsson turned away from Flemming to look straight at the army officer. "The goddamn Reds is my best guess, maybe some of the boys from the Industrial Workers of the World—the Wobblies," Karlsson said, nodding to himself. "They've been stirring the shit pot here since I don't know when. I'm not surprised in the least, to tell you the truth. Buggers have been agitating and agitating and no one really seemed to care a whit. Time to make a statement, I guess they figured, and here we are."

"Have you got someone in mind?"

"I've got all of them in mind." Karlsson smiled. "Just need to find the pick of the litter."

Chapter 3

1922

H. H. Flemming worked her way to the center of town, stepping along planks that spanned burned-out chasms where buildings had been. She stopped at Thiel's first and saw it was blackened nearly to oblivion. Leaning toward the rubble, she sniffed the air for the sour scent of kerosene, but the breeze kept her from identifying anything beyond the smell of char. Farther along Commercial Street she ran into Lem Becker, a gaunt, gray man from Tennessee who Flemming knew as the local agent for the Ku Klux Klan and editor of its paper, *The Western American*. She had met him in the spring after a fire near his offices along the waterfront and then had talked with him during her investigation of the Hammond Mill fire. He had a long face with perpetually wet lips that were as red and shiny as an apple. The man was unctuous. Rachel had taught her that word, and it fit.

"No pointy hat today?" Flemming asked.

"Afraid it might blow off," Becker said, extending his hand for a shake. "And they charge you double for replacements."

She pretended not to notice his outstretched hand and instead swept her eyes across the burned-out blocks around them. "You seem chipper today," she said.

Becker stuffed his hand in his pocket and surveyed the crumpled heap that used to be the Bank of Astoria.

"Any idea how this happened?" Flemming asked, then offered a long pause.

"No clue." Becker forced a smile. "But tragedy has a way of sowing many good things, don't you think?"

"Dunno." Flemming shrugged. "Mostly what I know is that it leaves behind a whole mess that someone's gotta clean up. A dead person or two as well. Hard to see the upside in something like that."

Neither budged for a moment, and Flemming finally turned to continue her tour. "Tell me if you find out anything in terms of the origins of this fire, will you? The state of Oregon would like to know."

"Indeed I will," he called after her. "Always happy to help those trying to right a wrong."

Becker's mood hadn't been as chipper as he'd let on. The November elections had taken a toll on his sleep habits. He'd had to do things he didn't want to do, but come January, the Klan would take over the mayor's office and most of the city council. Certainly the men at HQ in Atlanta had to be happy with that. The fire had made things better, maybe, but also more complicated, namely the poor sap found hanging dead at the end of Sanborn's.

Becker waited for the fire investigator to wander away and found Sheriff Harley Slusher in the pit of a collapsed street, helping the owner pull a stack of men's suits out from the rubble of a department store. The fire was still popping up in spots, but mostly the town was covered in swirling curtains of smoke and ash.

He motioned the sheriff over. "Listen, I've got a small thing that needs fixing. It's not much really, but we need you on this," Becker said.

Slusher wasn't tall, but he was thick with muscle beneath an oversized head that could only belong to a Swede. In July he'd been voted in as sheriff in a special election that Becker had engineered after the drunken tragedy at the Whistle Stop tavern. Slusher was a ship mechanic by trade and was one of the first to join the Klan after Becker came to town. He knew more about engines than the law, but Becker thought he had one of those faces that fit the job—especially his furrowed brow over close-set, obedient Spaniel eyes that left one wondering if he was mean or stupid or both.

"He's a bit of an oaf, isn't he?" Becker had asked the grand dragon, Fred Giffords, in his little Portland office as they hatched a plan to get a new, friendlier sheriff into office. Giffords was the Klan's top man in the state.

"Yes, of course he is, but he's *our* oaf."

Becker hadn't changed his mind much about Slusher, but the man was competent enough to get this problem dealt with. He told him to find the coroner, who would be busy and distracted because most of his office had been destroyed in the fire.

"Tell him you checked that body hanging at the Sanborn docks and that it looks like the sad fellow took his own life. Probably just scared to death seeing the town burn down. Tell him he can save himself the paperwork and a complicated coroner's inquiry and just list it as a suicide. A tragedy on a night of tragedies."

"I can do that," Slusher said.

"Tell him that the sheriff's office checked it out and it's all taken care of, except for the burying part. He'll still have to look after that."

Slusher nodded and began picking his way back down to the man he'd been helping in the burned-out pit.

Becker stopped him before he got to the bottom. "Sheriff," he called after him. "Plenty of time to clean up this man's mess. Let's take care of this other issue first. *Now*. Please."

Sheriff Slusher found E. B. Harrington at what was left of his funeral home. Half of the lobby was burned, most of its walls and ceiling gone—so the dim winter sun had been let in—and the floor was covered in a mix of paper, ash, mud, and dirty snow. Besides the fellow at Sanborn's, two other men had died during the fire: Norris Staples, a city council member who sold cars, had dropped dead while trying to push a Model T out of the fire's path; and a young Norwegian crewman on a tugboat drowned during the excitement.

Harrington, red-eyed and exhausted, was in a back room buttoning the shirt over the barrel chest of Mr. Staples, who was faceup on a table, stiff, and without shoes. The sheriff told the coroner about the man found hanging beneath Sanborn's. Harrington nodded without looking up.

"I'll do the paperwork but won't be before next week," Harrington said. "I know very little about the fellow, just that he was from Olney and had come down for the night. Do you have anyone who witnessed him take his life or heard him talk about such a thing?"

"I do," the sheriff said, pausing to drink in the sight of poor Norris Staples, hoping the lie found purchase. "I'll get that to you before you start your forms. Shouldn't be hard."

The sheriff took a step toward the door, unsure if the conversation was quite over.

"Just odd that a man would kill himself right when the whole city is burning to the ground," said Harrington, who was now knotting a brown tie around Staples's neck. "A person tends to seek out a peaceful place for their final moments. That's been my experience, Mr. Slusher, and I have occasion to visit a share of suicides."

"Well, it was a troubling night for all of us. I suppose some people are just better equipped to handle excitement than others."

"True enough."

The coroner patted Mr. Staples's chest and straightened the tie under the man's chin. "Sold me an automobile two years ago last summer. Still runs like a champ," he said, finally standing up tall to face the sheriff. "But, returning to the matter at hand, this dead fellow from Olney. Get me that witness report when you can, would you?"

Flemming stopped by the coroner's office late the next morning. They'd met before; the last time was over an arson in Seaside where a young man had razed his uncle's shack in an insurance scheme but failed to notice his uncle sleeping inside before he set the fire. The boy, only nineteen or twenty, was so distraught he'd tried to cut his wrists with an ink pen while Flemming was interviewing him at his father's hardware store. She took pity, wrote up the cause of the fire as "likely accidental," and the young man wept at the act of charity.

"You're looking fine, inspector," Harrington said with just a glance.

Flemming was wearing an outfit she was fond of: military-grade wool pants that she'd been given by a friend of hers who had been in the war—he was roughly her height but heavier, so she had to cinch the trousers with a belt high on her waist—and a pair of leather lace-up boots that nearly reached her knees, plus her overcoat and hat. From afar she could be mistaken for a man who perhaps worked in the forest.

"How's business?" she greeted the coroner.

"Too goddamned brisk," Harrington answered, unbothered by the clouds visible through the blown-out roof that threatened to send rain into his office. "You'll pardon my lack of civility."

Harrington was sitting at his desk where piles of ash-covered papers were weighted down with rocks, shoes, and heavy books. Flemming eased onto a wooden stool opposite, and the coroner let out a long sigh.

"Three dead from the other night: heart attack, drowning, and possible suicide," Harrington said.

Unprompted but apparently for her benefit, he ran through the details of each in a monotonous recitation of names, ages, times, places, bodily dysfunctions, and likely causes of death. He'd been county coroner for almost twenty years now, subjected to an unending blur of calls in the middle of the night, countless forms to fill out, bodies to paw over alone in the quiet of his office, and feigned looks of concern and sympathy for the families. By now the daily business of death had been reduced to a series of simple mechanics and transactions. He was a fisherman before he was elected coroner and had never spent much time contemplating all the ways a person could die. Now the list was longer than he cared to recite: pneumonia, stillbirth, tuberculosis, murder, heart attack, automobile wreck, brain hemorrhage, drowning, unspecified disease, choking on a chicken dinner, industrial mishaps of the most gruesome sort. People dropped out of existence as easy as a penny into the river, he'd come to learn. Some of them even seemed in a rush to see what was on the other side of the black curtain. These three dead in the fire, well, it was hard to say how they felt about death, and it was much too late to ask.

Flemming scribbled notes and let Harrington expectorate the particulars of each dead man. As the coroner wrapped up, he pulled a brown glass bottle from somewhere inside his desk, held it between his knees, and uncorked it. "Do you mind?"

Flemming made a point of checking her watch and offered a half-smile. "I'd never begrudge anyone their medicine, no matter the time."

"Amen to that," Harrington said with a smile. He pulled out two glasses and they shared a long, silent drink as the wind sent a few papers fluttering to the corners of his desk.

"Not bad at all," Flemming said, finishing her glass. "This suicide the other night. It's funny . . ."

"Can't say that I don't find it unusual," Harrington agreed, refilling both their glasses. "But you'd be surprised, Inspector Flemming, by what happens in our final moments. We sometimes find ourselves in the most peculiar predicaments, I must say. This poor fellow—the one at the Sanborn docks—it's difficult to tell exactly what might have happened. The sheriff tells me they've got someone who can attest to this fellow's despondency ahead of his demise."

"Ah." Flemming nodded. She took another deep swig and let the warm glow wash over her neck, face, and ears before it settled in her belly. "Despondency."

They drank another glass together, and soon a light mist was falling into the office.

"I mentioned peculiar circumstances," Harrington said after a long quiet stretch. He rifled through a stack of papers and found what he was looking for. "Perhaps you read about this fellow back in January, down at the docks. Ericksen was the name. They were loading coal onto a ship when the poor bastard got his arm caught in the drum of the crane. Yanked it right off like you'd pull the leg from a crab. The rest of his body followed, straight into the spool wheel. Crushed his skull. Just like that, he's gone."

Flemming laughed for a second—a combination of the booze and the terrible, awful absurdity of this man's end.

"A few weeks later," Harrington continued, his voice now stammering a bit, "a few weeks later one of the net-menders, a deaf fellow, drowned his wife in a rain barrel over near the Youngs River. Held her upside down by the ankles."

He stood up to demonstrate but wavered on his feet and slouched back down in his chair. "Then, when was it, April? This Japanese man at the

Hammond Mill . . . he fell into the grinder. Lost his balance and fell . . . do you know what a grinder is, Inspector Flemming?"

"Never had the pleasure," she said. "But if it's anything like it sounds—"

The coroner cut her off as he dug into another pile of papers. "A grinder is a wonderful machine. It spins around . . . let me see here. I've got it written down here in my notes . . . yes, it chews up bits of wood that they don't need at the mill . . . here it is."

He settled into his chair and read aloud. "This is from my report. 'The manager informed me the grinder was made up of 32 three-inch knives that spin at 720 revolutions per minute. It slashed his body into such small fragments that no one could determine whether it was a human body, other than by a hand and other small pieces of the body and clothing mixed with sawdust and small pieces of wood.'"

Flemming moaned and felt a little sick. "Oh, good lord."

The coroner took a small, drunken delight in the fire investigator's reaction and found another report on his desk. He sipped from his glass and went on. "And then did you hear about this man? A Chinese fellow called Go Yet was shot seven times as he came out of the toilet. Can you imagine?"

Flemming got up to leave, unsure how much longer the coroner would spend recollecting the city's death cases if she didn't move along. She wobbled on her feet and drew in a long breath of winter air to clear her head.

"It seems you can't take a shit anymore in this town without . . . without . . . and now this . . ." Harrington trailed off, looking up at the sky and the ruin of his office and the rain coating the two of them and the papers spread across the desk. "I hope you'll pardon me, Inspector Flemming. Terribly indelicate of me, of course. The circumstances of this week. Well, regardless, it's no way to speak to a woman." He let out an exhausted sigh.

"It's no way to speak to anyone who isn't in your awful business," Flemming replied.

The coroner stood and tried to collect himself. "Do you suppose this is hell come upon us? Have we been that bad?"

Flemming made her way to the door. "Not sure that's for us to say, Mr. Harrington. But I do thank you for the medicine."

Sheriff Slusher returned to Harrington's office later that day and gave him a typed and signed statement on department letterhead from a witness who said this hanged man seemed distraught the night of the fire, mentioning something about losing his week's pay at a card game.

"Who is James Barnes?" Harrington said, reading over the single sheet of paper. "Your witness?"

"He's a fisherman from Ilwaco. He was in town the night of the fire. Said he ran into your fellow that night. It's all there."

"And one of your deputies took this statement?" Harrington figured it for a fake—if the sheriff wasn't crooked, he was at least a little bent, the coroner had come to believe.

"It's all in order, Mr. Harrington. You should be happy to have one less dead man on your rolls awaiting processing," Slusher said. Then he leaned in, awkwardly craning his head down toward the coroner like a tall bird probing for a drink. "That's not liquor I smell, is it?"

"I don't think so."

"I hope not. We've seen what happens when a county official gets mixed up with the wrong people," the sheriff said, standing straight again. "Forget about the Sanborn fellow. The point is that he's dead. Nothing changes that now, not even an official declaration by the Clatsop County coroner."

It was a clumsy attempt at coercion, but the coroner decided to leave it be.

Chapter 4

1899

The first time Bart Layton saw Astoria, in the spring of 1899, the city was only a string of dim, flickering lights across the Columbia through four miles of foggy darkness. It was a place to be ignored or at least avoided as often as possible.

"It's full of rotten men and rottener women," his mother had said on his first boat ride with her across the river to pick up boxes of books for her school back in Knappton, Washington.

Once they'd picked up his mother's supplies, they stopped in the mercantile to get a few groceries and then walked straight back toward the little ferry that had brought them across the river. The people didn't seem particularly rotten to eight-year-old Bart, but they were loud and rude. As they left the mercantile, a man with a salt-and-pepper beard appeared out of an alley, put his arm around Bart's mother, belched like a roaring lion, and nearly fell over in drunken laughter. Back on the boat Bart could tell his mother wanted to say something but didn't and instead kept one hand on her hat to keep it from being blown out to sea.

Bart woke up two years later to find his father gone from their one-story house backed against the woods on the edge of Knappton. He'd never been particularly interested in Bart or his sister, Viola, and apparently wasn't that interested in their mother either. He'd run off to Tucson to work in a silver mine and was shot to death at a bar a few weeks later. His mother had found out in a letter from an Arizona sheriff that she read aloud once to the two children and then tossed into the stove.

"He had a problem with most folks," their mother told them over dinner that night. "God knows we all tried to help him onto the right path, but he was too stubborn, or too sick in his mind, to know better."

She paused to poke the sheriff's letter deeper into the fire.

"Your father was complicated, but he wasn't a bad man," she said and left it at that, adding after a long silence when Bart's mind had long since wandered, "Maybe he has peace now."

Bart's dad had worked at the Knappton lumber mill but never more than a few weeks at a time. Bart mostly remembered him sitting sullenly around the house, a dark cloud perpetually in a state of near-bursting. And when he did burst, it was bloody, either for his mom, his sister, or himself.

Bart didn't miss having him around, though he felt like he should have. Viola sometimes asked her brother what their father was like, but Bart didn't have much to say.

A year after their father died, Bart carried out his first burglary, when he was eleven. He'd been walking home from school and saw a neighbor's house with the door open. At first he just meant to close it but then, after calling from the threshold to see if anyone was home, stepped inside. The sensation of intruding into a forbidden world sent a tingle through his body and left his fingers twitching as if they were controlled by someone else. The house was nicer than his own and he was careful not to touch anything, keeping his hands clasped behind his back and his ears attuned to any noise of someone returning home. He went from room to room like that until he stopped in the dining room at a shelf with a set of porcelain place settings out for display. They were white with blue etchings of the countryside and windmills and kids in mittens sitting on sleds or making snowballs. Idyllic scenes of winter-bound harmony. Bart took a long breath and picked up one of the saucers for a closer look, turning over its cold form in his hands. A dog barked somewhere outside the house. Bart jumped, stuffed the saucer in his coat pocket, and ran back out the front door, leaving an orphaned cup on the shelf.

The theft sent a charge through him. He kept the saucer under his pillow for a time and took it out at night, studying the scene, tracing over the lines and cracks. The pleasure, he came to understand later after years of thieving, derived from possessing a forbidden object and harboring it when no one else knew where it was, if they knew it was missing at all.

Things began to disappear in Knappton. Buttons and bits of silver-ware at first, and hardly anyone noticed. When watches were nicked from dresser drawers and caps were taken from their pegs, tentative murmurs rippled around town until they'd risen to the ears of Ben Cart, a company man sent from Seattle to make sure the mill was choked with trees and workers were cutting, stacking, and shipping the lumber off to Japan and China as fast as they could. He was a fearsome man but on no occasion a drinker, so his temper never rested. Cart, whose patchy black beard sometimes became the butt of jokes behind his back, rode the men at the mill hard but believed in a sense of fairness, once even threatening to quit when his bosses in Seattle proposed cutting wages in Knappton after a flood had washed out some of the forest roads, slowing production by half one winter. The men earned their wages squarely, so it agitated Cart to hear their belongings were being pilfered.

One morning he opened the window to his bedroom and then snuck into the woods nearby to watch his house. He missed three days at the mill like this, crouching among the ferns, quietly sipping coffee, and waiting. Finally, late one afternoon while he was peeing on a Douglas fir, he saw the back end of the boy squeezing through the window. He found Bart Layton deep in his armoire, rustling through his coats and pants like a raccoon in a garbage pile.

On Ben Cart's orders, Bart spent the next day sitting at a table in the community hall with his stolen wares on display, and, one by one their rightful owners came by to reclaim them, some silently, some with a laugh, more than a few with a tongue lashing. They all knew Bart, and they all knew his mother, the teacher at the schoolhouse.

"This is what a low person looks like," Mrs. Gregg told her young son as she took back her hat pin. "You ought to be ashamed, Bart."

He had been ashamed initially, but that wore off as the day wore on. After a while he was just bored and perhaps a little proud that he'd managed to find his way into so many homes for so long without getting caught. Ben Cart didn't see the charm. He walked Bart home in the rain that night and snatched his ear in one of his cold, meaty hands.

"This'll be ending right here," he said, twisting Bart's ear hard. "Your mother deserves better than a thief in her house. She's got enough to worry about."

He wrenched Bart's ear another quarter turn and almost lifted him off his feet. Bart yelped, but Ben Cart didn't relent just yet. "You and I will have a serious problem if we don't put this to bed right here, tonight," he hissed. "Clear?"

Two nights later there was a fire at a storage barn at the mill, and most people in town were there either to watch or make sure it didn't spread. Bart Layton was inside Ben Cart's home, pocketing a gold watch chain and a pair of spectacles.

The next fall, instead of starting the school year in Knappton, Bart was sent north to the reform school for troubled boys in Monroe. His mother wept when he left but provided no protest.

The school in Monroe wasn't so much for reforming boys as it was for keeping them out of trouble and away from most people. With its high fences and locked doors, it was more of a prison—a place for young offenders "warped in morals," as they said. Monroe was a barely-there timber and dairy town about thirty miles north of Seattle, but the prison, ashen and foreboding, gave it a sense of grim permanence.

The closest Bart Layton came to reforming was refining his art of larceny. The guards, among the best-paid workers in town, were rewarded for their vigilance over their wards. There was a two-dollar bonus for catching anyone stealing from the prison's supplies and five dollars for foiling an escape. The system became a money-making scheme for the guards, often pretending to catch young boys in the act of some crime or another, collecting their cash while the young offenders were sent off to a darker, colder wing of the facility.

Bart tried several times to steal a set of keys from the guard's desk but lost his nerve each time, scared by a premonition that he'd drop them on the concrete floor and give himself away. His bunkmate, a needle-nosed boy named Will who'd come to Monroe after rolling a homemade explosive into a café in Olympia, goaded him.

"You're as good as what you do, not what you say," Will said after Bart told him the story of robbing Ben Cart. "Everyone's grandfather was a war hero or saved a woman from a burning building or caught the biggest fish or killed the baddest wolf or robbed the most banks. I believe what I see."

"I know what I've done and what I've gotten away with," Bart preened. "And besides, I wouldn't be in here for nothin', would I?"

"Some guys are in here for a lot less than they say. That's my only point," Will said, acting bored. "Talk is talk and doin' is doin'."

A week later Bart was caught stealing a set of pens from the guard's supply closet. He heard the guard's yell from behind, but as he turned, a wooden club thundered across his cheek. The blow sent him sprawling on the closet floor, an explosion of color washing across his eyes. That night in the infirmary he had a dream, or maybe it was a vision, of a girl he went to school with in Knappton, Asta Blomquist. She had brown hair and gray eyes, except in his dream her features were cast in a yellow glow, not angelic exactly but otherworldly. In the dream they were walking arm and arm through the forest and she was coyly nudging up to his ear, saying something sweet that he could never make out. He woke up in tears with a warm, longing ache high in his chest.

Breaking out of Monroe wasn't hard. The back gates opened up every Monday morning to let the grocery truck in. Bart feigned sickness on a Sunday afternoon, settling in for the night in the infirmary. When the orderlies went to bed, he pried open a steel cupboard with a thick metal ruler, took the keys that got him into the main building, and made his way, door after door, to the loading area in the back. He spent a rainy night in the firewood box near the gate and walked out in the dark when the grocery driver unlocked the back gate and drove in.

It took five days to get back to Knappton, most of it on foot and a few stolen rides on trains, sneaking bits of food along the way and sleeping in a wool blanket he'd taken from a house the first morning in Monroe. He was surprised his head still hurt from the beating he'd taken, alternating between flashes of blistering pain behind his eyes and a dull ache that never really went away.

His mom hugged him when he stepped through the back door into the kitchen, ran both hands through his curly dark hair, and then pushed him back. "You're not supposed to be back yet. What are you doing here?"

He unraveled a long story about doubling his class load at the reform school and testing out early because of his good grades and improved behavior. His mom didn't believe him but also couldn't bring herself to send him away again.

"I've changed for the better," he insisted. "You'll see."

She thought it was true that something had changed. There was an ugly mark on his cheek—roughhousing with the boys at Monroe, he'd said—but there was something else. A light had shifted in his eyes and left something hollow behind them, something that was difficult to read and even more impossible to reach. Maybe he'd matured in his time away, developing the first inklings of distance that men put between themselves and the rest of the world as a protective mechanism. It could be that, she reflected as she puzzled over it in the ensuing weeks. He'd been gone less than a year but maybe this was how mothers started to lose their sons.

Bart took a job with a logging crew, cutting and stacking slash, and came home each night to be schooled by his mother and sister. No one from Monroe ever came looking for him.

With his father gone, a string of men cycled through the house, loggers with thick hands who mumbled through their stubbly faces and spoke to Bart only when his mother was in the room. By the time he was fifteen, Bart was nearly as tall as most of them and raged silently at the lusty parade of visitors—shamed that his mother would let so many inside their home (though she seemed to take up with very few of them) and furious at the confidence these men carried, certain they were entitled to something that didn't belong to them. One night during supper, one of the suitors barged through the door drunk in sopping wet clothes. Bart tackled him around the waist and drove him back out through the door, toppling into a wood pile. The man, the brother of the chief of Bart's logging crew, was built like an ox and quickly gained the advantage. He climbed on top of Bart and was beating his head when his mother came out and finally tore him off.

"Vile runt," the man said, swaying on his knees.

Bart grabbed a piece of firewood and swung it at his face, missing flesh and bone but catching the strands of his beard. It put a momentary scare into the man that flashed into anger. He drunkenly lunged after Bart only to pitch forward uselessly on his hands. Bart stepped forward and unleashed an awkward, weak kick into his hip, which felt like a slab of meat and gave no indication of injury.

"Ooh hoo," the drunk man laughed and then dropped his voice. "Try that again, boy, and we'll end this tonight."

His mother guided Bart back into the house and left the man lying in the dark of the spilled woodpile.

That fall, Bart pursued Asta Blomquist. She was a year older than him and had finished high school that year, making plans to go to dentistry school east of Portland up the Columbia River gorge in The Dalles. He'd been carrying her around in his chest since that dream at the infirmary in Monroe the night the guard clubbed him in the face. He'd rarely thought of the future but now he did, imagining nights with Asta, wordlessly feeding the stove in their own home while the winter rains poured down on the forest around them and they stayed dry and protected. The scene played through his mind again and again while he worked and ate and settled into sleep at night. They'd never exchanged any more than a few words in school—she was shy and he was awkward—but the thought made him ache until he thought he might burst.

He broke into the upstairs apartment that she shared with her aunt above the mercantile. They were both at a wedding at the community hall along with most everyone else in Knappton. He found her bedroom quickly enough and stole a few pieces of stationery from her desk and a triangular piece of broken blue glass that was dull on the edges like it had been scoured on the shores of a beach. He returned a few days later with a cryptic but affectionate note on her stationery, although he couldn't bring himself to include his name. She found it under her pillow that night and puzzled over it as she drifted off to sleep. Two more notes followed that fall before Asta left for The Dalles.

Chapter 5

1910

Arni Leino returned to Finland but only for a few years. Suomi was in the grips of deepening divisions. The White Finns, including his Aunt Olava, were rigid and religious and intent on keeping close ties to Russia. The Red Finns, his Uncle Remi among them, were Socialists with an awakening civic consciousness, who favored drink and goading their sanctimonious countrymen. Remi railed endlessly in favor of independence. Olava burned the Socialist newspapers and spat on them in the fire. It was a colorful but bitter dispute that never seemed to ease. Finally, arguing over dinner one night, Remi laughed so hard at his wife's red-faced protest against dancing that his chest seized up and he fell dead into his *kalakukko*.

When Arni returned to Astoria in 1910, Lily wasn't the same. Her eyes were perpetually red and watery, her nose ran, and she'd become shifty and paranoid. She reminded Arni of a domesticated animal left to fend on its own so long in the wild that it had become feral.

She'd fallen in with a tall, hollow-faced ex-sailor named John Black. He sold cocaine and opium in small paper packets to dock workers and, more often now, the growing ranks of loud and idle men and women who preferred dancing and carousing to work and hopped from one boarding house to the next, leaving rent unpaid and petty thefts in their wake. The back room of the furniture store where John Black worked hosted a procession of users who never seemed to quite have enough money to cover their purchase. There was a smaller adjoining room with a mattress where Lily sometimes lied with John in order to get a dose or two of narcotics.

"You're a mess, Lily. What would Papa think of what you're doing?" Arni asked when he found her stumbling around Thiel's Pool Hall one night.

"My papa isn't here and neither is yours, *veli*," she slurred at him, putting her face close enough for him to feel her sour breath on his cheek.

She made a mockery of primping and preening his shirt and coat and smoothing his hair to the side of his head like a little boy.

"You were always more put together, and, to be honest, I have admired that," she said, her voice still unsteady and eyes barely lit. "Not enough men in this town take the time to keep themselves up. It shows you have . . . you have . . ."

She wavered a bit and poked her finger into his chest as if to finalize her point but never found the word she was searching for. Instead she went back to her friends, laughing and dancing as she moved across the room.

With his arm draped over Lily one morning a week or two later, John Black offered Arni work delivering furniture and occasionally delivering his packets. Arni refused and watched John Black labor to conceal the anger on his mousey face.

"There aren't many wages easier than this," John Black said, while Lily swayed with hollowed-out eyes. "You'll make as much in a half-day here as you could in a week gutting fish."

He pulled Arni's sister closer with his hand around her waist but never took his eye off Arni, whose stomach had turned greasy and unsettled. Black grinned.

"You make a delivery, collect the pay, and leave. The customer is happy, you get paid, and the reliable movement of goods and capital continues. If you're a curiosity-seeker like your sister, you will visit every nook and cranny of this town, meet all sorts of unexpected people, upper-crusters—a judge and maybe a doctor or two—all the way down to those on the edge of the edge, eating the scraps of the scraps, if you follow. Good for anyone geographically minded too. You can't know a place until you've been through its back doors, alleys, and parlors."

Arni knew enough about Astoria that he didn't want to know more. Around each corner there were thieves, hustlers, pimps, bruisers, addicts, and all manner of corruption and discontent. The sheer salty darkness of the place, day or night, seemed to starve men of their better intentions and leave only animal instincts behind. He recalled something his father had told him one night not long before he died, when they were talking about Astoria in their cramped little room at the boarding house: "When you get to a place like this, teetering on the edge of the map, you get to feeling like you can get away with anything—that's how far you are behind God's back."

Arni didn't stay in town. He took a job at the logging camp in Olney, a tiny settlement in the woods about eight miles south of Astoria. The camp was run by an independent outfit that sold its cut logs to whoever was paying. The year Arni arrived, the money came from the Western Cooperage Company, which sliced and bent the Douglas fir and Sitka spruce into barrels for fish markets in Alaska and across the Pacific. He was brought on as a cook's helper, peeling mountains of potatoes and ladling stew for a few dozen tired men who seemed just as wet and sullen in the morning as they were at night after ten hours on the job. But after dinner the camp was alive with fires, arguments, bawdy stories, cards, drinking, and scuffles. Arni kept mostly to himself, watching and doing his best to stay out of the way.

Two men died in Arni's first month at camp. Some logs got away from a horse team on a muddy hillside one morning and crushed a Swede named Larsson. "The air was stolen from him so quick he didn't have time to say 'boo' before he was smushed, and that was that," a sawyer flatly recounted to Arni while he sopped up his plate with a biscuit the following morning. Not long after, a puckered little man who applied grease to equipment got very sick, but the foreman refused to take him into town. While the men were away in the forest and the camp was quiet, Arni watched helplessly while the grease monkey seemed to shiver himself to death sitting in the doorway of the bunkhouse. The foreman and the cook wrapped his body in a horse blanket and stowed it beneath a wagon for the trip into town the following week to hold a burial at the pauper's cemetery on the hill.

Arni became the grease monkey for a few months and then, as time passed, worked his way into some of the other crews. He helped the fellers clear a path into the forest and notched the trees the crew chief decided were ready to come down. The sawyers followed, bucking each tree to the forest floor and then Arni walked the length of each one with an ax, chopping branches as he went and taking care to keep his footing on the slick bark. The foreman chided his slow pace and he learned to move faster. A while later the road crew was a man short, so Arni joined them, helping to skid logs down the mountain. The lesson there was simple: do whatever needed to stay upslope of any tree moving downhill.

That was how it went: one job and then another. He discovered he had skill and strength—nothing extraordinary—and a knack for learning new tools and techniques and applying them without slowing the operation or getting himself hurt. For the foreman, Arni came to be a handy man to have around camp, someone to fill in the cracks in his operation when a worker went down with injury or slunk away drunk in the night.

Surviving in the forest required keeping one's eyes open, mouth shut, and mind alert. These were sopping, slippery, and primordial woods that had changed little in a thousand years and remained wholly uninterested in protecting a human life. To stay sharp, Arni drank tea and coffee every chance he could. During any lulls on a shift, he stepped away from the crew and walked deeper into the forest, places where ancient ferns reached his chest and logging noises gave way to cottony quiet. The rain fell more often than it didn't, and the smells were intensified with each new washing of the woods. The bark gave off its own musky odor and the wet soil underfoot reminded him of rotting bread. When he looked up, droplets pelted his cheeks and eyes, sometimes obscuring what he thought might be owls perched on branches, watchful eyes that seemed wary and unperturbed at the same time.

Best of all were fleeting moments in the late spring and summer when the clouds disappeared. Yellow shafts of sunlight would stab through the canopy like a foreign force and find their way through the trees and onto the forest floor. Suddenly what had been murky became clear, if only momentarily. Mosses and ferns erupted into vibrant greens and grays, almost violently bright. Craggy tree trunks rippled with shadows. Lichens, barely considered by anyone passing through, revealed themselves as a wonder all their own, living patterns on the bark with their own secret story to tell. Even the fog on the branches, caught unexpectedly in the sunlight, seemed to come to life as misty particles separated and went their own way. Arni saw the forest illuminated like this several times a year and it always stopped him short. The feeling was something like delight but also an ache at knowing the moment couldn't be captured and would vanish before it could sear into his memory, unable to be fully recalled later when it was greatly needed.

The camp itself wasn't much. There was a main office, an indoor-outdoor kitchen, and a few long and narrow bunkhouses. They were hastily built things, assembled from low-grade timber and always leaning to one side, with a thin bench that ran the length of the wall—the men called it the deacon's seat—and beds set up end to end. Every few years the camp would move closer to the next tract of land to be denuded with axes, saws, and eventually a miraculous steam-powered engine called a donkey that dragged cut trees off the forest floor from places where horses or ox teams could never gain purchase.

New faces, too, came and went in the camp: Finns, Swedes, Irishmen, Italians, Germans. Arni picked up a few words in new languages, mostly those that aided in the work or avoided the kind of misunderstandings around camp that led to fights and sore feelings.

One year turned into five and soon became more, and the seasons put distance between Arni and his sister. They saw each other periodically, mostly when Arni came into Astoria for a dance or a night at the Louvre or the rarer occasions when Lily happened to be at the Olney store and café with a group of visiting friends who thought the place and its rugged occupants, with their corked boots and shortened pants, were exotic. Sometimes, especially when there was no sign of John Black, Lily looked good: fresh-faced and ready for anything. *Still just a child turning her face to the sun*, Arni thought. Other times she was haggard and lost and smelled like those who sometimes had to sleep out in the rain when they ran out of money.

Arni found a rhythm of the work in the woods that seemed to divide itself into two over the course of the year: the rainy season and the not-quite-so-rainy season. His life found a center at the camp and in the work. He liked the heft of the axe and the two-man saw, along with dual feelings of pride and melancholy when they felled a monster of a tree with a "whumph" and a rush of air that rattled their clothes and made them holler for some reason.

Nights in the bunkhouse were harder. Arni missed his sister and she played in his thoughts as he drifted into an exhausted sleep. At times she showed up in his dreams, a helpless figure in peril or exploding with laughter so loud that his eyes snapped open in the dark of the bunkhouse. Either way he was left with a lost, cavernous feeling in his chest that he often brought with him into the forest the next day.

Chapter 6

1922

A rumor that one of the newspapers printed after the fire caught H. H. Flemming's eye. A woman—the story didn't mention a name—claimed that just before the fire started, a dark-haired man came into her room and said he'd just started a fire downtown. "You'll see soon," he said. Fifteen minutes later the town was lit up.

It sounded a little made-up but seemed worth checking out. *If it happened, it would've happened close to where the fire started at Thiel's,* Flemming figured, *at least within running distance.*

Astor Street was busier than usual when she arrived. Flemming was happy to see that many of the legitimate downtown businesses displaced by the fire had to temporarily relocate to Astor Street, right there among the bootleggers, opium addicts, crooked shops, and the working women. *Self-righteous do-gooders can always use a dose of seeing how the rest of the world lives,* she thought. It was late in the evening—no sense going down there in the day when no one was awake—and the street was buzzing with the commotion of the last few days.

She knocked once on an unmarked wooden door that she knew and then stepped into the darkness. The stench of beer found her first, followed by the noise of bottles being stashed in drawers, under tables, and little cutouts in the walls.

"This isn't a bust. I'm only here about the fire," Flemming said flatly, unsure of how many people she was talking to. "And maybe to quench my thirst a bit."

Once her eyes adjusted she recognized the woman behind the table off to her right. Liz had been in Astoria ever since she could remember. She ran a couple illegal bars and had a stable of rotating girls that Flemming had played cards with, betting with cigarettes on nights when their money and work were scarce.

"Well, looky here. If it isn't the cutest fire marshal on the West Coast," Liz said, opening her face into a small smile. "I wondered how long it'd be before you showed up."

She poured Flemming a beer from a big glass jar that required two hands. It wasn't cold, but Flemming took it in with one long drink and pointed at the empty glass for a refill.

"Thirsty gal," Liz teased. "You're gonna need it. But weren't you supposed to be married by now? Last I saw you, you were on your way to wedded bliss with, what, an insurance broker, wasn't it? He had one of those simple, flat names. Bob or Ron or Dan or Don."

"Tom. And he was an asshole."

"Oh my," Liz said, straightening up in mock astonishment. "Stop the presses. Something happen?"

"Only that he thought every open bedroom door on the block was an invitation and he couldn't bring himself to decline them," Flemming said.

"Well, if you're never home and chasing every whiff of smoke that happens to turn up, there's bound to be—"

"Don't start. Or else be prepared to fill that glass a few more times," Flemming said. "Anyway, he's someone else's problem now. I supposed you heard this entire town burned down?"

"Is that so?" Liz smiled. "Yes, moving on to more pleasant things, I see."

Flemming pulled out the newspaper clipping with the story about the woman and the strange visitor and tapped her finger on it. Liz read it over while Flemming finished the second beer, feeling her spirits begin to rebound after discussing Tom. Her sister had pegged him a shit heel from the start but she'd stubbornly pressed on.

"Who was this?" Flemming asked. "A fellow comes into some woman's room and says he's lit the town on fire. Was it one of your girls?"

Liz narrowed her eyes and Flemming, finally adjusting to the dim light, noticed that her friend's hair, swept into an efficient nest atop her head, showed a few signs of gray.

"Not that I've heard. And I think I would've heard. Then again, there are a lot of girls I haven't seen much of since the fire. Some ran off to Portland and a few of them owed me money, which doesn't please me much."

"Have you heard anything about how the fire started?"

"Same as everyone, what I read in the papers. Wobblies, socialists, Reds, maybe the everyday miscreants at the pool hall."

"But anyone specific?"

Liz leaned in closer across the bar and glanced around the room. Flemming was suddenly aware there were others in there too, vague figures in the gloom clustered two or three around a table. Liz refilled her glass and pointed with her pinkie to two men sitting at a table against the opposite wall. "The guys from the Finnish paper, the *Toveri*," she said quietly. "About as Red as they come."

"What are they doing here? The union hall didn't burn, as far as I know."

Liz's place typically catered to fishermen, loggers, local businessmen, and the occasional cop. The Finns had their own underground drinking halls, so it was odd to see two of them here, calmly sipping from their glasses. Flemming paid up, crossed the room on wobbly legs, eased herself into the open wooden chair at the Finns' table, and introduced herself.

"We can talk to you but not here and not today. Tomorrow," the smaller one said. "At the east marina in the morning. A boat called *Marie*."

They both stood up to leave. Flemming rose too but swayed like a Doug fir in a stiff seaward breeze. By the time she put her hand out for a shake, the men were at the door and then gone.

The *Marie* was moored at the far end of the marina. Flemming found the same two men from Liz's inside the boat's cramped cabin, along with a third man who was a half-head taller. All three were standing around silently with their arms folded as if they'd been waiting all night for her to show. The *Marie* reeked of salt water and fish but, judging from its unseaworthy looks, hadn't been a fishing boat for a long time.

Flemming put herself in the only empty corner in the cabin, folded her arms the same way, and let the quiet of the marina, only broken by the impatient noise of gulls, sink in.

"Fellas," she smiled, hoping to clear the fog of the previous night. "Good morning to you."

The tallest of the three, who only had a few inches on Flemming, looked at his compatriots with dismay and said something she didn't understand. One of the others responded in English. "Yes, a woman," he said derisively. "Have you not seen one lately?"

Flemming nodded in confirmation at the taller one. Most days she tired of the routine of self-explanation. It required an exposition about how her father had been a fire inspector, first in Ohio and then in Portland, before joining the state fire marshal's office. No, he hadn't gotten her the job. Yes, he had taught her a good many things about how fires start and especially about the people who started them. She'd been a volunteer firefighter in Ashland while attending Southern Oregon Normal School with plans to become a teacher. Her father heard that an assistant state fire investigator, a man named Tubby Franks, had died of a heart attack while investigating an arson at a milliner's in Corvallis. She took the test, applied, worked her way up, earned her promotions by solving cases, and now, in her late thirties, had a well-rehearsed self-history to recite about how she, a woman of all things, had come to be investigating this fire.

"I'm Paulo," the third said to Flemming and then nodded at the other two. "Jorg. Ring."

Paulo and Jorg had been in Liz's the night before. She would've remembered Ring, whose wool sweater and coat both seemed a few sizes too small. Flemming thought he looked like an overexcited loaf of bread attempting to escape its sack.

"Does your husband know you're on a strange man's boat?" Ring asked with a greasy smile.

"Does yours?" Flemming retorted.

Ring pouted as the other men laughed. When they grew serious again, Flemming forged on. "Thank you for meeting with me. I must say, there have been abundant rumors around town about this fire. And if you'll allow me to be blunt, some of them have landed right here."

No one seemed surprised at the accusation.

"This is tragic. There is no avoiding that," Paulo began; his English was clipped and darkened with his Finnish accent. "But I've seen what they've been saying about us, and it just isn't true. I know people want to believe it. Our branch of the Finns has caused an upset in Astoria for certain. But something like this? No. It's too much."

The other men nodded solemnly at the floor and kept their arms tightly folded.

"I will also say, if I may," Jorg started in with a high nasal voice that surprised Flemming. "We remain steadfast in our goals and are certain that we are right that the existing economic systems benefit none but the most powerful and enriched. A disruption at the highest levels of the largest scale is indeed needed to trigger those necessary foundational changes we must have. And yet, yet . . ."

He paused to finally look up and see Flemming rolling her eyes as the boat gently rolled beneath their feet. "This is not something we called for or advocated, not in the *Toveri* or in our meetings."

"Because you find it repugnant?" she asked.

"Because we find it of limited benefit."

Paulo leaned forward and sniffed.

"We have no problem with the fire. In fact it has perhaps begun a process of re-examination for this city's wealth structures," Paulo said. "One can hope at least."

"Maybe so, maybe not, and I'm not sure I care. For the moment though," Flemming said, "it's being pinned on you. Well, not you per se but the Reds . . . or some sort or another. The Wobblies maybe or the Finns. It won't make much difference to them."

"They would love that. I'm sure of it," Paulo said. "I've only been out of prison for a few days, haven't I? Come back to town to take my revenge on the city that arrested me, tried to destroy my paper, and sent me away for three years?"

Flemming's mind wandered. She wondered if the big Finn, Ring, had ever been with one of Liz's girls. She had sometimes overheard them talking about the meaty bulk of some of their customers, men who couldn't seem to help but knock over lamps, block doorways, and leave other men in a bruised pulp in the wake of a conversation gone sour. Ring may have been one of those bumbling kinds of brutes, but an arsonist? It was hard to figure. Flemming struggled to refocus on Paulo's words.

"I could give you a long list of people who might've started that fire," he continued, "but I don't suppose you'd have much trust in that, would you?"

"I don't suppose I would," Flemming said, "but let's try anyway."

Chapter 7

1922

Despite the not-so-subtle warnings from Sheriff Slusher, E.B. Harrington spent more time than usual examining the body of the man found hanging the night of the fire. *A coroner's job*, he sometimes reminded himself, *is to know death, inhabit and understand it, and assign it a cause.* Motivation came and went, though, so he found he had to muster extra effort sometimes.

Not this time.

Harrington decided to call Slusher's bluff at least once. He rang the sheriff not long after his first visit and asked him to return to the funeral home behind the YMCA. When the sheriff arrived, Harrington motioned him to the table with the man's body and hunched to show the bruises around the sides of the man's neck. Since the fire, his body had been wrapped in a bolt of burlap and stowed in the cellar, kept cool by the unusually cold weather.

"I'm troubled by what I see here, sheriff, I must say." Harrington touched the dead man's neck with his fingertips. "These kinds of acute dermal abrasions and discolorations aren't consistent with ropes."

The sheriff leaned in closer as the coroner's fingers poked and prodded.

"Not at all," Harrington went on. "The angle is wrong. The stress in these markings should be up and down—following the gravitational pull and friction between the man's own body weight and the rope. Had he died from hanging, these marks would be altogether different. Different indeed, I dare say, sheriff."

Both men straightened up. Harrington wiped his hands with a discolored handkerchief and continued his ruse: "Now tell me again about this witness your deputy spoke with who was positive this man died from self-inflicted strangulation by way of hanging. Please. Otherwise I fear we're on the verge of a homicide investigation."

Harrington's diagnosis had left Slusher shifting from foot to foot next to the man's gray, partially undressed body. The coroner had no idea whether the marks on the man's neck indicated anything about anything, but his speech seemed to have done its job; the bruises made this lawman nervous. Slusher moved quietly toward the door, unsure of what to say.

"You have your paperwork and your witness statement," Slusher said finally. "Nothing here changes that."

In the end Harrington relented. He had no idea what had happened to this poor fellow except that he'd been found dead at the end of a rope at Sanborn's dock. *But who hangs himself when the whole city is burning to the ground? And who bothers to carry a rope all the way down to the docks on a night like that?* Unsettled as he was, Harrington filled out the form, noting the cause of death was "self-inflicted strangulation," and put his signature at the bottom.

Part 2 *Fuel*

Chapter 8

1908

It was Bart Layton's mother, Anne, who found love in the winter of 1908, when her boy turned seventeen. Ole Estoos had arrived decades earlier, back when Knappton was still called Cementville on account of the rock quarry that was set up not long after the war between the states. He came just as the limestone grew scarce and business turned to the trees that grew on the hillsides around town. He was one of the first hired to help clear roads to get the fir, spruce, and cedar out of the woods and down to the new mill on the north shore of the Columbia.

At first the timber just went upstream to Portland and Vancouver. As years went on, though, bigger ships came from Asia: four-masted beasts with massive holds and foreign men who swarmed Knappton's piers once the ships were tied up. It was even busier across the river in Astoria, where the port had become a frantic hub of shipping and trade. As coal and cut trees moved east on ships and furniture, rugs and other luxury goods arrived from Japan and China, destined for Portland and points farther inland.

The inbound ships also brought sickness and deadly disease. An inspection station briefly occupied Astoria but then was moved across the river to an old salmon cannery in Knappton. Ole helped build the Columbia River Quarantine Station on the timber pilings in Knappton Cove during an exceedingly rainy fall and winter in 1900, then stayed on as an employee. Foreign and outbound ships were still inspected in Astoria, but those suspected of harboring sickness were immediately sent over to Knappton. Once docked and sealed off, huge copper pots of sulfur were lowered into the holds and left to burn until the fumes

had killed everything aboard, rats and fleas among them. A yellow flag
went up on the mast once the ship was deemed safe. Meanwhile sailors
and passengers were inspected for cholera, influenza, malaria, smallpox,
yellow fever, and leprosy. Healthy sailors were sent back to their ship.
Those suspected of being sick were stripped, deloused, and quarantined
in tents or stowed aboard an old gunship parked at the docks. The lucky
ones were sent to a one-room dorm on shore called the "pest house." The
stay could last weeks or months, determined either by visible improvement or death.

Ole worked as a ship fumigator and then, when the sulfur headaches
nearly debilitated him, he advanced to quarantine manager and finally
top man at the station. He and Bart's mother had known each other
for years—casual acquaintances in their small community—but only
recently had become friendly. Ole was a hard-working, decent fellow
who treated Anne well enough and even offered to get Bart a job at the
quarantine station.

"Sailors may be sick but at least they're not as ornery as those boys
at the mill," Ole said.

It was a hard point to argue but Bart refused, denying Ole the pleasure
of employing the son of the woman he was pursuing. Ole and Anne
eventually married in Astoria and bought a house on Franklin Avenue
with a view of the river. Without a place to stay in Knappton, Bart left too.

He found his way to The Dalles that summer and watched outside the
dentist school for Asta. At the end of the second day, he saw her leaving
with a group of students, a wool coat tied at her waist and a bundle of
books under one arm. She was engaged in a serious conversation that
Bart couldn't make out, but the sight of her almost made him sick to
his stomach. He spent three more days watching the small campus,
alternating between a bench across the street from the main entrance
and a path he wore out that circumscribed the block.

"Don't be a fright," he said to himself but stayed anyway. The men
who had pursued his mom back home, before Ole, had taken the same
predatory approach, he recalled, lurking from afar until they thought

the time was right. The piece of blue glass in his pocket turned over in his fingers. *This isn't like that, and I'm not like that.*

At the end of the fifth day, with the winter light starting to die outside, Bart went to the lobby of Asta's apartment building and waited in a tall, padded chair next to a table with magazines. Asta came in alone, struggling to hold a stack of books that was in danger of spilling onto the floor.

"Uh, hello," Bart said, standing up, surprised to hear his knees crack so loudly in the lobby. She was as pretty as he remembered but older and a bit more world-weary than the girl he'd known in Knappton. She didn't recognize him at first, but then his face finally registered.

"Oh, hi," she said, getting her belongings under control. "What are you doing here? It's Bart, right?"

He smiled that she knew his name and felt his ears go warm. Of course she did though, Knappton only had a few hundred full-time residents and they'd only been a year apart in school.

"I was in town seeing a friend," he said. "Actually, I was here to see you and, uh, see how your school is going and what you think about becoming a dentist."

Asta stood still, puzzling over Bart and trying to decide if she should be scared.

"Is it good? Is it something you want to do?"

"I think so," she said, unsure where the conversation might be going. "So how did you find my apartment building?"

Bart did some quick calculations over the value of explaining that he'd been circling her in The Dalles all week. Better to avoid that altogether.

"There was a dentist, from Long Beach, I think, who developed serious misgivings and quit a few years ago and ended up moving to Saskatchewan and now he's working in a train yard." He paused as she started to laugh. "He might've been from Ilwaco, but he definitely ended up in Saskatchewan. In Canada."

"So," she said, putting her things down and crossing her arms, "you're here to save me from Saskatchewan?"

"It's horrible up there."

"I happen to be an amateur scholar on Midwestern Canadian provinces and have it on good authority that it's quite tolerable. Long, cold winters notwithstanding."

"It's filled with dentists who regretted becoming dentists," Bart retorted. "Excellent teeth all over town but unhappy people, every single one. That's what I've heard."

He convinced her to eat dinner with him. Years later Bart tried but never could remember what exactly was said during the meal except that he told her about Monroe and Ole Estoos and a vicious fight that he'd seen in the woods back home between two sawyers and how one of the men died and that Bart helped drag his still-warm body into the pond where it was sunk with a pair of rocks tied around the man's waist. She talked about The Dalles and the arrangement of teeth and how she was the only girl in her class and the boys that tried to impress her and how they'd been allowed to try experimental anesthesia, a gas that you inhaled and made you feel like you were floating three feet off the ground. He sensed she was holding back, though, guarding something valuable he couldn't get to, maybe a place reserved for her secret, most important feelings and thoughts. Love might even live there. He promised himself that, given time, he'd be let into this inner chamber. A good burglar, he knew, must be both patient and opportunistic.

Bart left The Dalles with her address in his pocket, promising to write, feeling like he'd breathed in two tons of that gas she'd mentioned and wanting more.

Not long after, he took a job in Tacoma as a bellhop at a hotel called the Union Club. He wrote letters to Asta on hotel stationery, lying that he'd been staying there during an apprenticeship with a lawyer. He was fired from the Union Club after a few months for stealing from the guests. The police roughed him up, splitting his lip, and drove him to the train station still in his bellhop uniform. The Union provided enough money for a train south to Vancouver but nothing more. The city, perched on a slope on the north shore of the Columbia just across from Portland, was rife with unlocked doors and easy-to-open windows. A fifteen-year-old boy in grubby clothes gave him a tour of downtown late one night, pointing out the buildings' weakest transoms and which back doors were occasionally left open by cooperating shop workers. The small network of pinchers gave him a cut of the action, provided that he shared half of what he stole. In exchange he got a room in a ramshackle house, some cash, and meals cooked by the woman who ran the house.

Bart slept during the day and worked in the predawn hours stealing coats, knives, hats, suits, and even fish from a market near the river. He turned nearly all of it over to a man named Jenkins, who waited for him at the house each morning as the sun was coming up, paid him cash from his pocket, and whisked away the goods. Bart never bothered to ask what became of them. He was happy to be building a small roll of money that he kept in an envelope in the closet of his room. A few months later he caught a new recruit in his room searching beneath the mattress. They fought, and the woman who ran the house kicked them both out.

Jenkins refused his goods the next morning. Two days later Bart was arrested coming out of a department store with a handful of women's furs.

"A little birdie told us we might find you shopping this morning," the cop said. He was sentenced to eleven months at the State Reformatory in Monroe, not far from the boy's school. The judge pressed him to sell out his cohorts in exchange for a lighter sentence, but he refused. "I'm a thief but not a rat," Bart told him. Worse, the news made *The Oregonian*. It was a small item buried on page thirteen, but he wondered if Asta saw it. He'd written her once from Vancouver, explaining that he'd found work as an office clerk. Before the trip to Monroe he begged one of the officers to let him write another letter.

"My girlfriend will be worried to death," Bart insisted, but the man just smiled.

"No, son," he said. "One is more than enough."

Eleven months stretched into almost three years at Monroe after he joined a group of men who tried to escape one night after knocking out a series of lights and made a run toward a weakened piece of fence on the back of the grounds. Bart was expelled from the wing of the prison meant for younger offenders and put in with the harder criminals. That's where, over the endless winter hours that were dark and wet, he befriended a fellow burglar who told him any true professional needed training and only one man—a German fellow in Butte, Montana—would do.

Prison was difficult, and the chill of the stone buildings and shiftless men had left something cold in him. He'd become not only more weary but more suspicious of those around him. And there was something else: Early on in prison, especially at night before he went to sleep, thoughts of Asta had provided a slight sense of solace, just enough to let him drift off and perhaps not be troubled by dreams. As his stay wore on, his visions of her became blurred—he could no longer recall the features of her face or even be sure of the color of her hair. It troubled him to lose that mental image; it felt like he was on a ship watching a friend sink under the water and disappear into the dark. His mind and emotions became more frantic and more disorganized and knowing that only made him more so. The afternoon before he was released, one of the other inmates stole the biscuit he'd saved from breakfast. When he didn't protest, the man lit into him with a hail of punches. Bart let the blows fall on his head and face without defending himself, and he didn't know why.

Knappton was much the same when he returned. A timber crew gave him a job piling slash a couple of days a week. The company was bulking up, worried that the United States' fresh entry into the war in Europe would start sapping the young men in its ranks. Bart filled out a draft card in Knappton, half-hoping he'd be conscripted, go off to fight overseas, and later tell his heroic stories to Asta.

The first chance he could, he took the ferry over to Astoria to see his mother, Ole Estoos, and his sister, who was now a tall teenager. "Trouble does find you, does it not?" his mother said, touching his still-bruised face.

She shared gossip from back home—including that the quarantine station had almost been moved to Portland—who'd gotten married, who'd died, and who'd left in the night with the mill's payroll never to be seen again. He didn't recognize most of the names, but it didn't matter. She then mentioned in an offhand way that Astoria was getting its first female dentist, Asta Blomquist from Knappton.

"You remember her, right? She's a year older than you, isn't she? Always very bright, as I recall, and a very nice girl. I didn't know she was interested in teeth," she said, smiling to clack her teeth together. "Very modern of her. Has her own office downtown."

Bart broke into the Bee Hive department store two nights later. He'd taken the last ferry over from Knappton and spent most of the night in Thiel's Pool Hall, getting a little drunk and trying not to be conspicuous. His mind had been swimming ever since Asta's name was mentioned, sending him into a state where every subsequent conversation felt like it was coming through a dense and distorting fog. He had gleaned that Asta had an office on Commercial Street, in the third story above the Bee Hive. Since she was a new dentist, a Dr. Barnett had agreed to allow her into his practice in the hopes that she could take over when he retired in a few years.

It wasn't hard to get in. There was a landing on the back stairway where he stacked two milk crates and hoisted himself through a bathroom window. It was late by then, maybe three in the morning, and most of the city was dark and quiet, save for a few opium dens where muted orange light snuck out from behind drawn curtains.

Once inside, he climbed the stairs and found the dental office door was open. Bart walked around slowly, taking in every detail in the dim light, thumbing through the ledgers, picking up pliers and scrapers, and running his hands over the furniture. There was an embossed letter on the wall certifying that Asta had completed dentistry school a few months earlier. There were two patient chairs near the front windows overlooking the street. They were complicated things, with a spinning seat to adjust the height, adjustable arm and footrests, and circular pads to lean back and rest your neck. Bart climbed into one of them, opened his mouth, and imagined Asta hovering over him, staring deep into his face, concentrating solely on his well-being. It was easy to imagine ascending into heaven that way, he thought, just floating up and up as the world fell away. He fell asleep in the chair and woke as the first dull slivers of summer daylight angled onto the street.

"Shit, shit, shit . . ." he sputtered, tripping over the footrests as he climbed out of the chair.

The drop out of the bathroom window to the milk crates on the stairs looked too dangerous to attempt, so he found the interior stairs that deposited him in the back of the Bee Hive. Unlocking the front or back door to leave seemed risky at this point—hadn't he done that time and again in Vancouver?—so he decided to stay put. He hid in a dressing room in the back for several hours until the store opened and he heard customers shuffling around, chatting, and starting their day. When the din was right, he left the dressing room, smoothing his hair and putting on a face of a normal browsing customer, and showed himself out. He realized on the ferry it was the first time he'd broken into a building and left without something in his pocket.

He went to the Bee Hive three more times over the next month, following the same late-night routine except that he scavenged a short wooden ladder from the docks that he used to climb in through the back window. He allowed himself just a few minutes of dreaming in the dentist's chair—but no sleeping. The third time, he took an armful of women's coats from the Bee Hive and two cops were waiting for him at the bottom of the back stairs. He was dazed and bewildered when they took him to the station and booked him.

"I can't seem to stay out. I don't want to stay out," he told them when they asked how many times he'd been in the Bee Hive.

"Are there other coats? Who were you selling them to?"

"It's just those," he said. The prospect of going back to prison sank into his neck and shoulders and his throat tightened up. "It's like Jonah and the whale. I want the whale to swallow me, but it won't. It keeps coughing me back up and won't let me stay. Why won't it let me stay?"

"The Andersons are decent people and have run that store for a long time," said one cop, confused but not curious enough to follow up. "They don't want you there, and they certainly don't want you stealing their things. The good news for them is that it's going to be awful hard for you to come within a whiff of their place from your cell at the rock pile."

Bart's brain cleared long enough to register the cop's face as one of the men in Thiel's drinking a couple of weeks back, out of uniform and ornery. The other one took him by the arm and showed him toward the city's tiny holding cell.

"This way," he said, "*Jonah.*"

Bart was soon sent by train to Portland, where the police had agreed to hold him until his trial for the Bee Hive break-ins. Five days later, in the middle of October 1917, he climbed through a loose panel in the ceiling of the Portland jail and down a drainpipe to the street.

A cellmate in Portland had pointed him toward Butte, Montana, and a German named Count Schneider, a sort of master thief who traveled the country imparting his wisdom to those willing to learn and share a portion of their bounty. So the story went, at least. Bart had been warned about Butte, and the Count was no angel either, but he went anyway, unsure of what else to do. The police in Oregon were no doubt looking for him, and it was no use going back to Knappton or Astoria or even Vancouver. He hitchhiked to Seattle, spent two nights at the railyard, and finally hopped an eastbound freight train headed toward Minneapolis. He was in Butte the next day and soon enough slogging through the layers of wet autumn snow in the city the locals called "the richest hill on earth," on account of the copper deposits underfoot.

The streets were still buzzing over the hanging of Frank Little that summer, a brazen murder of an out-of-town Wobbly who'd come to Butte for a miners' strike, just weeks after more than a hundred men had perished in the disaster at the Speculator Mine. No one had been arrested. Talk was rampant that the copper company had strung him up, or maybe the Pinkertons or the local cops or even rivals from other unions. "A dirty deed. Six men snatch a fellow in his skivvies in the middle of the night and take him across town for a neck party at the trestle," a fellow train-hitcher told Bart as they walked through the railyard. "Butte does that to you, though. Watch yourself."

On his second night in town, three men pulled him into an alley near the library and put the boots to him. He had no money to give, so they took his hat and coat.

"We'll come for your trousers if we see you again," said one man with an Irish brogue as he slung Bart's coat over his shoulder. "The day after that, we take your shoes. And if we find you without shoes, God help you."

Another snowstorm arrived the next morning, covering the city with heavy flakes that stuck to his shoes and the cuffs of his pants. It would've been beautiful if it wasn't so cold.

He met a woman named Digger Haynes when she caught him stealing carrots from a load of produce being delivered to her restaurant in Meaderville, one of the city's ramshackle neighborhoods. Rather than call the police—Butte was exploding with so many hungry and depraved men, would they care about a carrot thief?—Digger approached him with a butcher knife and a smile.

"I could feed you those carrots and maybe a few of your own fingers too," she said. "Are you that hungry?"

Bart liked how her brown hair hung like a gauzy curtain over her eyes. She peered out like she herself was hiding something. She was at least ten years older than him and had the look of someone ten times as tough, he figured.

"I am that hungry, miss," Bart said, putting the carrots back on the stack he'd taken them from. "But hunger comes and goes; it comes and goes. And I can feel it going already. I think I'll follow it right out of here if it's all the same to you."

Digger took a step closer and dropped her smile.

"It doesn't really work like that. You've already committed the sin against me and my establishment. You don't get to absolve yourself too. You don't decide that."

Bart smiled. "Would you like me to pray with you, then?"

"I'm no believer. Exceptin' . . . I do believe I have a mountain of porcelain plates that need to be scrubbed, and my dishwasher walked out on me a few hours ago."

He washed dishes at Digger's for two weeks, sleeping on bags of onions and potatoes in the back and eating scraps from the plates that came back from the front room. He and Digger talked often, usually in the lulls between shifts letting out at the mine. Her parents were missionaries who left for China when she was fifteen, and now she only heard from them in letters. She worked at the restaurant as a teenager and took it over after the owner collapsed into a snowbank during a late-night booze run and froze to death. There was a man she was in love with, but he'd died in the Speculator Mine disaster a few summers back, she said. "One of 166, how's that for you? Probably drowned when they turned off the water pumps. That's what the government report said anyway, but who can believe those?"

Bart told her about his thieving and his arrests, leaving out the part about escaping from the Portland jail, instead emphasizing that his were mostly harmless crimes, that material goods had their own lives, and that no one person should hold on to any one thing forever. Digger rolled her eyes.

"Spoken like someone who hasn't had to work for anything they bought."

The remark hurt, and the pain only deepened when he finally asked her about how he might find Count Schneider.

"Your line of work, I suspect, really has no masters. They are all small men like you who are desperate to do something without actually having to do anything," she said but cut it with a smile. "Capable of big things, no doubt, but still small people. Like all of us, I suppose. But there is no Count Schneider here. If he was, I would know it. I probably wouldn't tell you where he lived, but I'd tell you if he was here."

The next night, still stung by the conversation, he told her about Asta and about how she'd never returned any of his letters. Digger probed him deeply about her, her family, Knappton, the dental school, what had been said in The Dalles, how Asta seemed, and what hints to her real feelings there might've been in what was left unsaid.

"Prognosis not good," she said with a wave of her hand. "Given multiple chances, a woman will show an interest. It'll be in her own way, but it will happen and you'd know it. And you don't know it because it hasn't happened and it's not gonna happen. That's the sad truth of it, and I'm sorry to put it so plainly."

Two afternoons later, despondent and sick, Bart went to the dry goods store in the middle of town, stuffed two bags of rice in his coat, and walked out slowly into the winter sun and waited. He was arrested a few minutes later.

Chapter 9

1917

It was in the woods that Arni Leino first began reading the *Toveri*. It showed up in the latrines and on the floor of the bunkhouse and sometimes folded mysteriously beneath his pillow when he returned from a long day in the woods. It was good to see so many words in his native language. He had worked on his English ever since he'd arrived in Astoria, but he still dreamed in Finnish. Reading the paper was like feasting on a dessert from back home.

Not that there was much sweetness to be had in the words. The *Toveri* picked and poked at the scabs of the unrest that had consumed Suomi back home and nourished those bitter divisions for those who'd come to the United States. The newspaper's history was well-known in the camp and around town. It had started in Astoria in 1907, back when the city had more Finnish immigrants than any other city west of the Mississippi. The first editors were veterans of radical politics in Finland, feverish embodiments of the socialist movement trying to carve out a political system that went beyond the root-bound, church-going Finns who seemed only too happy to leave every injustice in place on Earth and let God sort it out later. Or so said men like Santeri Nuorteva, a balding biscuit of a man whose fluffy exterior hid a burning flame ignited by anyone who disagreed with his voluminous editorials on the front page. "He is a jackal and comes from a family of jackals," he told an underling once, regarding a member of the Astoria City Council after he complained about something or other. "Everyone knows that, and he will never change until his back is to the wall. Which won't be long from today, I'll have you know."

Nuorteva, like so many at the helm of the *Toveri*, had a short stint in the editor's chair. In January 1913, during a meeting of timber workers at Suomi Hall, the local Shingle Weavers Union decided to expand and become the International Union of Shingle Weavers, Sawmill Workers, and Woodsmen. After the vote, Nuorteva stood at the front of the crowd atop a wooden crate and praised the decision, adding almost as an aside that the American Federation of Labor would be "a most important ally in strengthening this newfound union of workers."

There was a groan from the crowd—the American Federation of Labor had opposed the strike of mill workers in Puget Sound a year earlier—and a group of men with long memories pressed toward Nuorteva. "The IWW has twice the balls and four times the muscle!" one of them shouted. A deafening shouting match ensued in the hall and escalated into a brawl. Nuorteva was stabbed in the thigh, dragged out the back door, and left in the rain, his tenure at the *Toveri* over.

Predictably the next editor spoke nothing but praise for the Wobblies and their tough tactics but exited a few months later when he was caught with the typesetter's wife in a woodshed attached to the office, wearing one of her undergarments on his head. And so it went, a rotating cast of editors coming in and out of the newspaper as the rank and file—as well as the paper's stockholders—tried to sort out which labor organization to back. Sometimes the transitions were peaceful, sometimes they were adjudicated during fights that began in the *Toveri*'s tiny office and often spilled into the street. But the paper remained relevant and often deeply influential both in its reporting—the *Toveri* had correspondents in Finn-strong U.S. towns from coast to coast—and through its relentless editorializing in favor of workers' rights, unions, and the dismal failure of the capitalist system. It was strongest in the Pacific Northwest, especially in timber towns, and Astoria remained its epicenter of power.

Beyond the Finns, few in Astoria took note of the *Toveri* until the late stages of the Great War. It had mostly been printed in Finnish, and few bothered to translate it for the non-Finns in town. But the Russian Bolshevik Revolution in 1917 offered a fresh infusion of passion and excitement—the Marxist prediction of the collapse of capitalism was perhaps finally taking hold. "The poisoned lungs are taking their last breaths," the paper editorialized. A shipyard strike in Seattle, which soon made its way to Astoria's Tongue Point shipyards, added one more inducement to boldness. The *Toveri* began printing two editions—one in Finnish and the other in English—as a way to visibly support the striking workers, many of whom were not Finns.

"Those who wax fat with predatory wealth do so with the sweat wrung of the toiling masses," the paper wrote in a front-page editorial. "Ample working conditions and the right to organize know no nationality or country pride. We intend to do everything we can to support those endeavors and urge all others, by whatever means at their disposal, to join this historic struggle for the fate of mankind."

The edition printed in English caused a stir in Astoria. For many, it was the first time they ever knew the content of the little foreign newspaper they'd seen around town for so many years. To the uninitiated worker, the *Toveri* became a beacon or at least a sign that the labor movement had one more strong ally. Not long after, though, the windows of the office were broken and a note was left inside. It read: "We are watching every utterance you make. Astoria already has too many people like you so take this fair warning to cut your anarchistic stuff and do it at once, or we will take care of you. First and last warning."

In the years that followed, the *Toveri*'s offices were routinely vandalized, advertisers were boycotted, and the U.S. government began an investigation that culminated in the arrests of its editors, publishers, and business managers—men hand-picked by the Finnish Socialist Federation. "Inciting rebellion" was almost always the charge—easily provable via circumstantial evidence and incendiary enough to draw a sentence of several years in prison. As paranoia over the "red menace" grew, so did the net for suspicious characters. Police rounded up anyone handing out socialist or communist propaganda—sometimes even anyone who absently took the handbills distributed on the street. Incentives went to those who ratted on their neighbors and friends. Sometimes it was cash, other times it came from a wooden sap to the shins. Either way it worked, and the crackdown soon expanded beyond political troublemakers. Once prohibition was in full swing, the jails filled with an assortment of men and women: bootleggers, radicals, Wobblies, prostitutes, killers, pimps, gamblers, hangers-on, and anyone else deemed an enemy of civil society in Astoria, Oregon.

The response was no surprise: the best labor organizers went underground, and those building the political resistance found their revenge in fires and bombs that destroyed businesses deemed unfriendly to the cause. Rocks were thrown through the windows of the chamber of commerce, often with the names of the imprisoned written across them in black letters.

"We have an untenable and unproductive tumor that is growing and spreading," the mayor told a secret meeting of businessmen. "We will, and must, excise this festering wound before it becomes septic."

Arni Leino had no intention of being part of any socialist movement, but he did find himself down at the offices of the *Toveri* on an autumn day, not long after the shipyard strike had begun in the fall of 1917. A man had come to camp to tell him that his sister had been discovered nearly dead at the river's edge at Smith Point, not far from Uniontown, and had been brought to the newspaper office. He hitched a ride into town on a logging truck and found her asleep under a pile of blankets near a man setting the type for the next day's edition. The office, a downtown building that had been a dairy barn in its previous life, was warm, and the air rippled with the smell of fresh coffee.

"She's lucky," came a scratchy Finnish voice. "The temperature's falling, so she might not have seen sunrise."

Arni turned to see a square-jawed man in a gray suit with big lips and a bandage wrapped once around his head. He touched it when he noticed Arni looking.

"There's been a bit of trouble," the man said casually, "but nothing that won't be dealt with."

"What happened to her?"

"One of our people was fishing from the shore and nearly fell over her as he walked back toward town. It was like she was in some kind of state that couldn't be broken. I'm told our man roused her with a few slaps to the cheek, enough to get her eyes open and mouth moving at least, and brought her here when she started speaking the mother tongue."

Arni bent over his sister and shook her shoulder. She only groaned and seemed to fall into a deeper sleep.

"You're from Suomi, yes?"

"Yes," Arni said. "It's been a difficult time for her. She's become mixed up with the wrong people, I'm afraid."

The man reached into his pocket and removed a brown paper packet, no doubt from John Black.

"Precisely," Arni said.

"I hate to see one of our family succumb to such influences. We've seen that only too often in recent years, and none of us are immune to its affliction," the man said. "She'll be safe here for a couple of days, and there are women who can bring her back to health. At least long enough to leave on her own strength. I'm Matti Sauso, by the way. I run the presses of the *Toveri.*"

Arni introduced himself and said he was grateful for any help with Lily. He explained that he worked at the timber camp in Olney and would pay for any help that his sister might need. He wrote his name down on a slip of paper with a two-dollar IOU note.

"Please," he insisted, "please do whatever's needed for her. My means are quite moderate, as you can imagine, but I will pay what needs to be paid in order for her to get well."

He remained kneeling next to Lily and searched her face. There was color in her cheeks, thankfully, and a steady draw of breath.

"She will be fine in a day, maybe two," Sauso said. "We take care of one another."

Arni returned to Astoria the following Sunday. He'd packed a lunch for them and told her they were going to walk to the top of Coxcomb Hill, high above town. She began to whine but relented—figuring it would probably be good to breathe some fresh air. They didn't speak much as they made their way past the colorful Victorian houses, the high school dug into the hillside, and finally through the thick woods that gave way to a steep meadow. They were both panting hard by the time Arni threw their bundle of food onto the grass and collapsed alongside it. Lily quickly joined him, and both were on their backs under a shifting cast of rain clouds that had yet to release their moisture.

"Are you okay, *sisko*?"

"I'm fine, veli," Lily said, turning her head with a sad half-smile. "Actually, I'm not fine. You know that."

He nodded.

"I miss Papa," she said.

He reached for her hand and found it, cold and skinny. They laced their fingers together and felt a soft breeze blow across them. Family blood stirred in both of them. They'd been in Astoria for years now but had lived separately for too long, their stories unfolding without the context of their shared ancestry. Arni felt that absence now and wondered if his sister, in her distressed fog, felt the same. Finally they sat up and began to unpack the food that Arni had brought.

"Lutefisk?" Lily laughed, holding up a partially unwrapped package. "Really?"

"We're celebrating," Arni said, and Lily laughed again.

"Oh really? Celebrating that I've made such an ungodly mess of myself?"

"Celebrating, sisko, because you just survived the tug of death."

Lily grew quiet, then murmured, "I suppose I did. You can look at it that way. But maybe I missed an opportunity to finally see Papa again."

"There will be plenty of time for that. Why rush?"

Just overhead two seagulls drifted past them, and one of them let out a loud cry. Arni and Lily lifted their heads. Arni was struck by the view from this hill, the behemoth Columbia to his right, the mouth of the river and the Pacific to his left, and forested hills in the far distance. An old-timer in Olney once told him there were enough trees in the Northwest to build a ladder to God and back with enough left over to build halfway to the devil, "or the other way around, depending on your fancy." Arni shifted his gaze and locked on to a place far out to sea.

"I don't want you to be around this John Black character any longer. It's not safe. I want you to go home." He let out a long sigh. "I want you to leave this place and go home."

"Are you forbidding me?"

"I would never do that and you would never agree," he said. "Do you remember the stories that Papa told us about the *hiisi*?"

"The troll?"

"Worse than a troll, remember? It was a version of hell that the hiisi carried inside him, spreading it to everyone he befriended. Remember? All who came to know him died in terrible ways. And quite quickly."

"Those are stories from the old country, veli. Things people say to scare children and keep them from finding trouble."

"This whole place is like that," Arni said, sweeping his arm across the city below them. "It's hiisi."

They ate for a long time in silence and didn't bother to move when a light rain began falling. Arni stole glances at his sister's face. How was it so carefree when all he could do was worry? When the food was gone, they began walking downhill. When they reached the edge of the woods at the bottom of the meadow, Arni stopped and turned to face her.

"Please, just think about what I asked."

She rolled her eyes and laughed a little, the same way she did when they were kids and he would caution her about walking across a frozen stream when winter was weakening into spring. "Yes, big brother. Anything you say."

Chapter 10

Montana's prison at Deer Lodge was the coldest place Bart Layton had ever been. The granite walls, built by the prisoners who came before him, seemed to capture the cold and reject the heat with no regard for the season. It only mattered at night, though. Bart spent nearly every day of his sentence on a work crew, building roads, cutting trees, constructing buildings, or working on nearby ranches. It cleared his mind and put a layer of muscle on his body that he'd never had before. Best of all, he had a small hand in building the prison's theater, paid for by William A. Clark himself, one of the copper kings back in Butte. One of the men he worked with, a mucker in the mines, forever talked about the murder of Frank Little and that he knew the identity of the men who kidnapped him from the boarding house before stringing him up on a railroad trestle. When the man wasn't talking, he was composing a never-finished tune about the iww and Little, its martyred rabble-rouser.

In idle moments Bart wrote occasional letters to Digger and let his mind find its way to Asta. On good days he found perspective and a little peace knowing that she was not interested in him and probably never was. When he was tired and dispirited, his thoughts turned angry and confused. Powerful imaginings of long periods when he and Asta had been a couple and had taken trips together manifested. He seemed to remember sitting on a wooden stool in her dental office with an armful of flowers, watching and whistling happily as she tended to her final patient of the day so they could go to dinner. His chest swelled at the thought and his eyes watered. *We were in love. We were building a life. What went wrong?*

When he got out of prison the last week of January 1922, he returned to Butte and got a job assisting a hod carrier. The city seemed to have an endless appetite for brick buildings and always needed more men—mules, really—to carry the bricks from one place to another. It was difficult, mindless work, and Bart stayed only long enough to save money to take the train back to Portland and then Astoria. Once the train crested the mountains and chugged toward the coast, he took a small delight in seeing the yellow skunk cabbage and daffodil blooms that seemed to announce that the coldest, wettest months were over and the gentler rains of spring had taken hold.

In Astoria he found the house on Seventeenth Street, blue with white trim, built to look a little like some of the ornate Victorian houses a few blocks away but cheap enough to be missing the finer details. Ole Estoos answered the door, but Bart's mother pushed him out of the way once she heard his voice from the front step. "Bart! My God, where have you been?"

He'd never written her from Montana. The papers had carried the news when he broke out of the Portland jail, and that was the last she knew of him. Bart spent the rest of the night alternating between accounting for his whereabouts since he'd escaped Portland and apologizing to her.

"No son treats his mother that way," he said, shaking his head. "You've always been good to me and deserve someone who treats you better than that."

Despite his sentiments, Anne Estoos saw a change in her boy. He was more haggard than ever, and she supposed a year in a Montana prison would do that. But his brain and his emotions were different too. She worried when she heard him say things that weren't true, things that had never happened except in the interior of his mind. He told her stories about what he and Asta used to do when they were together, like how he taught her to fish when they lived in Knappton. He laughed, recalling things Asta had said, like when she joked that his hair was so curly the robins would mistake his ringlets for nests and would someday begin depositing their little blue eggs on his head.

"She just has this way of talking . . ."

The more tired he became, the more he rambled into incoherence. But what never changed was the absolute belief in what he was saying. The certainty in his eyes never wavered, no matter how much his mother questioned, trying to sort out the difference between what her son was saying and what she knew to probably be true.

Bart heard his mother and Ole arguing that night as he fell asleep but made no attempt to follow their conversation. The next night Ole Estoos took him to a secret place on Taylor Street for a drink. Ole still worked at the quarantine station and knew several men inside the bar. He guided them to a quiet corner with two beers in large copper mugs.

"You need to know something, Bart," Ole said before taking his first sip. "You won't like it, but you need to hear what I'm saying and take it to heart."

Bart sank into his chair a bit and felt the air heat up around his body.

"Asta Blomquist got married last year to another fella. He's a good man. I know him, and I know that he's going to treat her right. They live here in town. They work here. They're going to make a go of it—"

"Married?!" Bart's voice rose.

"Yes," Ole said quietly. "Now, I'm sorry that I had—"

"I don't think that's correct," Bart said, setting his jaw and staring straight into Ole. "And I think you know it's not correct, so you can . . . so you and my mother can punish me for this little Montana episode. I said I was sorry for that and I am. But that's no—"

"But nothing," Ole cut him off. "I was at the wedding. I saw it happen. They're husband and wife in the eyes of God and the eyes of the law. It's done, and you need to be done with her."

Ole took a long drink of his beer and continued talking, but the words were drowned out by the blood rushing in Bart's ears. At the end of the monologue, Ole raised his cup for a grim toast. Bart reciprocated, out of good manners more than anything.

"To a new adventure," Ole said. "To finding new love, Bart."

It snapped him out of his fog.

"No, no it's not true and you know it's not."

He reached across the table, grabbed Ole roughly by the collar, and tried to throw him to the floor. The older man easily parried him aside and grabbed his wrist.

"I know that it is true, and you need to realize it. Tonight."

They drank the rest of their beers in silence. When they stepped outside, Ole turned back toward Seventeenth Street, but Bart went downtown. A white banner hung over Commercial Street announcing the summer regatta and couples spilled down the street arm in arm as a mist blew across the blocks. The front of the Bee Hive was locked, and he craned his neck to see if any lights flickered on the top floor. Behind, on the back stairway, the bathroom window was still open for anyone who wanted in.

Chapter 11

1917

Lily Leino didn't mention it during their picnic on Coxcomb Hill, but she'd developed a crush on Matti Sauso, the *Toveri's* handsome typesetter who'd been so kind during her episode. He delivered soup when she was tired and told stories from back home over coffee in the afternoons. When she asked about the bandage on his head, he waved his hand dismissively.

"A dog bite," Matti said.

"A tall dog, I'm sure." She smiled.

"Very tall. The kind that carries a rock and is ready to use it if you disagree about the value of human dignity in an economic context."

She met up with Matti several times in the month afterward. She learned he was bookish, a fine cook, a timid drinker, and a ferocious debater when it came to the fate of Suomi and the persecution of those advocating for the rights of all people.

"If we are not animals, we must be something better and we must treat each other as such," he enthused at the end of a monologue that poured out like a river, slipping from Finnish and English and back again. "And, I must tell you, history will regard this moment that we are in as a great point of decision for humankind, at least in this country. The fruits of fairness and equality hang within our grasp. We can pick them now if we have the courage, or we can let them rot."

He paused to see if she was still listening, and she was.

"Right now I'm afraid it seems we're inclined to leave them on the vine. It's very sad to me. In America of all places."

They slept together in his small, rented room in a boarding house at the far end of Uniontown. It was crowded with copies of the *Toveri*, pamphlets, and pieces of clothing that all had black stains from the printing press. The morning sun had a way of shining through the window that left Lily feeling like she was in a painting that she never wanted to leave. She'd gone days and soon weeks without any of John Black's packets or even John Black himself. It was both a relief and a source of bodily distress, as she fought to tamp the cravings of the warm rush that came with each ingestion. Matti could see her struggle sometimes and asked about it, but Lily lied every time.

"Just hungry," she'd say. "Cook me something?"

"Yes, of course, of course. Let's eat, and you'll feel better."

He was always sweet.

The romance lasted only a short time. One night while Matti was at the *Toveri*, Lily ran into John Black on Bond Street.

"Lily, it's been too long," he purred, taking her by the shoulder and guiding her into an alley. "I thought perhaps you'd gone off to Portland or some such thing."

She jerked her shoulder to free it from his hand and settled her back against a wall. He raised both empty hands above his shoulders, feigning innocence, and then made a show of putting them into his pants pockets. His face was smudged and now sported a scattered array of yellow and brown whiskers.

"Have you been good?"

"Good how?" Lily said, lifting her chin to look him in the eye.

"Just good. Have you been good?" His eyes darkened.

She didn't answer.

"I know where you've been, Lily. I know you've been warming the bed of that newspaper printer. Getting your fill of the Reds, are you?"

She cocked her head with a half-smile. "I've been better than I have in a long time."

"Well, that's a matter of some debate, I'm sure you'd agree," he said, making a point to run his eyes from top to bottom. "You certainly look like shit."

Lily started out of the alley, but John Black's hand was inside the neck of her coat and pulling her back before she could get two steps. Her back hit the wall and she grunted. She stiffened as he moved in close.

"As it happens, I know a thing or two about your lad at the *Toveri*. It seems his boys at the paper are fond of drinking and telling stories when they aren't out enlisting the world in their sad little revolution. The way I hear it, he's got plenty of affection and isn't afraid to share it with a good many other girls in town."

"That's a lie."

"Would you like their names? I can recite them if you like. There's Jenny down at the—"

Lily shoved him as her face reddened and tears welled in her eyes. She wanted to leave, but he blocked her escape with his arms and body.

"You didn't let me finish, Lily. There's Jenny at the bakery in Uppertown, the Dutch one with the big ass. There's a gal by the name of Margaret. She does laundry for the boys at the bar pilots' office. Quite pretty, as I hear it. The daughter of the owner of Owl Drug—her name escapes me at the moment, I'm sorry—but she's been a guest in his bed. I could go on . . ."

Bile rose up in her throat and she fought to swallow it back.

"I can understand your interest in young Matti. Sounds like you've got impeccable taste. Or, at least, common taste."

"Let me go," she said, letting the tears run freely down her face.

"It's time to end this little adventure of yours," he said, softening his voice. "I've missed you."

Just then she rammed her knee between his legs, sending him down on one knee and gasping for breath. A bit of rain found its way between the buildings and into the alley. John Black straightened up after a long moment, pulling one hand from his coat pocket, and before she knew it, he jammed his index finger into her mouth, and she instantly tasted a bitter powder on her tongue. He removed his finger and clenched her jaw to keep it shut until he knew she'd swallowed the contents.

"There," he said quietly. "There now. Isn't that better?"

She tried to knee him again, but he checked it with his other arm and leaned in to kiss her face, shuddering now as she cried.

"Shh. Don't do anything rash tonight. I'm leaving. I'm sorry I had to be the one to break the news to you about your friend. It's a terrible, vile thing to have to do. But trust me, it's for the best."

"Fuck you and fuck your filthy mother," Lily hissed, fighting the fog and euphoria of the drugs as they moved through her bloodstream and into her head.

He reached into his coat pocket, pulled out three paper packets, and slipped them in her hand, closing her fingers around them. "For you."

Chapter 12

1905

By February of 1905 it had been raining for months on end. Within the little house that Asta Blomquist shared with her parents in Knappton, grass was growing inside the door where a drip of water had crept in. They'd come from Des Moines and had never seen rain like this, endless water, and lashing and incessant storms that seemed determined to wash away their part of the world. Even the locals, whom Asta imagined had grown webbed feet over the years, seemed on the edge of madness. A dairy farmer had set off on foot in the middle of a torrent, leaving behind his family and vowing to find a dry bed in Seattle or die trying. Two brothers, lumbermen to the core, had simply decided not to repair the roof that had blown off their cabin and there were rumors that they could be found, day or night, sauced on homemade hooch and playing cards at their kitchen table as the rain poured in. One morning that month, not long after her twelfth birthday, Asta was at school when the hillside behind their house cleaved away, releasing a roaring sixty-foot wall of mud, rocks, ferns, and trees. Their house, hastily framed and shingled years before, was no match. It was entombed in seconds. After the slide was discovered, there were feeble attempts to unbury the house and rescue Asta's parents, who were presumed to be inside. A few hours of shovel work by a half-dozen men didn't seem to put a dent in the giant mound of debris that had swallowed her mother and father.

"It would be very difficult to survive something like this," a sad-eyed woman told Asta as they watched the men attempt to burrow inside. "I can't imagine there could be any air at all inside there, so how could they ever breathe?"

The men didn't even wait till dark to return home, that's how futile it all was. They promised to return to their work in the spring so her parents could have a proper burial, but no one ever did. The hummock of earth remained where it was, with no hint of what it hid, and by summer was covered in a fresh coat of sun-hungry grasses, ferns, and pioneering cloudberries.

Asta was left hollow by the death of her parents and spent several weeks after the landslide sleeping in the homes of her teacher, neighbors, and church families. Thoroughly numb, she refused school and most food, and it took all of her strength to be polite to those trying to help.

"Orphaned by the parents you knew is, frankly, worse than being orphaned by parents who'd never been in your life," said one man, a stranger whose home Asta found herself spending the night in, as they ate dinner by the fire. "But you may one day see it as a gift too. The time you had with them."

It seemed unlikely, but as days passed, she was able to begin considering another possibility: Had they found what they had been looking for, that mysterious force they believed would unite them with the rest of existence, no matter what side of time they were on? Asta could only ponder it for a few seconds at a time before her mind spun out in too many other directions—the infinity of time and the finality of death and the searing pain of loss.

Asta's Aunt Christine moved from Kansas to Knappton that April and they rented the top floor above the small mercantile on the main road. She had some money; Asta never knew how. Her aunt was sweet, well-versed in books, and devoured every magazine she could find. She was also quietly forceful when it came to her views about the treatment of women and the injustices put on them. Particularly galling was the denial of voting rights.

"We do twice the work at half the cost and somehow haven't earned the voice to participate in government," she said. "That may or may not change, I can't say for sure, but I know that if no one tries to make a change, it will never change."

"It's going to happen, auntie," Asta said proudly. She'd been reading the newspapers and pointing out every story where the women's vote was mentioned.

They got along well, and it was her aunt who ushered her through adolescence, helping with homework, taking her on trips to Seattle, and teaching her math, biology, and other subjects that girls weren't supposed to learn. As far as Asta could tell, her aunt knew more about more topics than anyone else in town. It was her Aunt Christine who pushed her toward dental school in The Dalles as her schooling in Knappton came to a close. Asta didn't object, neither to the fact that she'd be going to school with only young men nor to the idea of rooting around in people's mouths.

"The alleviation of pain is one of the highest callings possible," her aunt said, her face broadening into a smile. "Imagine what that will mean for the person in your chair. Imagine it. A brute of a man who fancies himself the strongest specimen in town who has to come crawling to a woman to free him from the bondage of a toothache. At that moment you, and only you, will control the future of his agony."

"That's not a very charitable approach, and I would never allow someone's pain to fester," Asta said with a laugh. "But there's no denying a certain deliciousness to it."

A few days before she left for The Dalles, Asta asked to go see the place where her parents had died. Instead her aunt took her to Peacock Spit, a long sandbar jutting into the mouth of the Columbia River from the rocky, tree-pocked headlands of Cape Disappointment, the southwesternmost point of Washington. The spit hosted a swirling mass of crashing white waves where the river spilled into the Pacific and the ocean pummeled the shore with walls of water that seemed to come from every direction. The waters could shift from deep to shallow in a matter of seconds, making it one of the most treacherous places in the world for anyone in a ship trying to sneak past.

They found a spot high above the spit where they could see how the vast expanse of calm ocean met the continent's resistive network of sandy beaches and sheer rock cliffs. Christine told Asta a detailed story about the USS *Peacock*, the U.S. government's scientific ship that had traveled around the world for years, only to founder and break apart at this spot within a few days in the summer of 1841.

"How do you know all this?"

"Oh, I read every silly thing I can find. You know that," she said dismissively. "It was a huge ship: eighteen cannons and all this surveying equipment and supplies. And then it was all gone. I mean some of it was salvaged, but most of it washed away. Except its bow . . ."

She pointed down to the spit.

"The bow is right over there somewhere, buried in the sand. You can see it sometimes if the waves pull back in just the right way."

Her aunt began a wandering monologue about the river mouth, a place pregnant with possibility and disaster no matter which way you were traveling. Somewhere the conversation veered into life, finding love, carving out a path through the world. Asta listened with only one ear because seagulls were swirling all around them in the high winds off the outcroppings, moving with a sort of dark poetry that put her in a melancholic trance. Her aunt talked on, and Asta felt herself get smaller against the sight of the heaving waves and wind.

"If you were to drain the ocean and the river right here, where we're looking, the wreckage you'd see would break your heart. So many ships and bodies just scattered all around," Christine finally said, putting her hand on her niece's arm. "But they were all out there, weren't they? Trying to get somewhere? That's what I always think about. Here they'd come to find passage through this terribly difficult place. Uncertain about exactly what awaited them on the other side but certain they had to try. Have to tip your cap to that, at the very least. Grim as it may be."

Dental school at The Dalles had been exactly as Asta suspected it would be. All boys and men, nearly all dismissive of her intrusion into their world, each hurt when she rejected their advances and then that hurt hardened into bitterness that was as durable as it was pathetic. She made a few friends but focused on her studies. Dentistry came remarkably easy and she took a perverse interest in how it attempted to marry modern medicine with medieval practices. Chemicals and hygienic protocols alongside pliers and devices that locked jaws into place.

The visit from Bart Layton had caught her off guard. They'd known each other in Knappton but only a little. After her parents died, he'd made a specific point to offer that his father had died too, but they were both kids and the conversation was unable to proceed much beyond a sad look they exchanged before the moment evaporated.

She was charmed by the things he'd said in the lobby and at dinner, but there were no feelings beyond that. Soon enough she'd pieced together that he'd been the author of the letters she'd received, as well as the anonymous note that had been left in her bedroom in Knappton. Each memory of a note fanned a tiny spasm of guilt because she could not reciprocate his feelings. It usually passed by the next day.

"Crushes are things that boys must learn to get over, like a rite to manhood," her aunt told her during a visit to The Dalles. "But their wounds never heal if they never scab over, so do him a favor and don't respond to these correspondences."

Asta kept the letters for a time. But when she moved to Astoria and became the first female dentist in town and soon married another dentist—a man named Frederick who was fifteen years older—she threw them away.

Chapter 13

1917

Not long before the war, the Wobs sent a man named Brewster to the forest in northwestern Oregon to agitate. He had a rust-colored mustache and a barrel chest. Nicks and scars scattered across his hands and face testified to a life of conflict and long odds. He was mean even to the workers he was trying to help.

"You like sleeping stacked like cordwood in your bunkhouse? Scuffing at mealtime like whelps fighting over a teat? You're toiling at the whims of managers who've never known a day of labor in their lives and wouldn't know an axe from a shovel. Six days a week, eleven hours a day with the rats and fleas at your toes when you come back to camp at night. Rotting, you all are, in the gears of capitalism and you haven't the foggiest notion," he hissed over a fire at a secretive gathering behind the logging camp in Olney. "You're pitiful excuses for men. I've seen women and little children do more to improve their lots rather than you all, lying over and holding your ass in the air, waiting to be mounted by these savages. You get whatever you think you deserve."

There were a dozen or so Wobblies in Clatsop County, professional-grade arm twisters and pamphlet pushers married to the insurrection—so long as they continued to be paid. Most of the men at the camp in Olney agreed with Brewster: Who didn't want more pay and decent meals and bunkhouses where the walls and floors weren't rotting through? Few dared to say it out loud, though, lest they take an axe handle to the ribs from the union busters hired by the company or find themselves suddenly abandoned in the woods without a job or even a way to get back to camp.

The forest men split over the best way toward self-improvement. The typical unions argued for a bit more pay and a few less hours, demands that seemed reasonable amid the current state of affairs. The Wobblies scoffed at that—"no man sates his thirst with a thousand tiny sips," Brewster had said—and instead called on a wholesale dismantling of the capitalist system to be replaced with one where the workers seized ownership of the lumber yards, mines, factories, and ports from coast to coast, no exceptions. The means for enacting that revolution might well be bombs, fires, guns, and bare knuckles. For starters, though, they needed at least an expression of interest from the men on the ground. Brewster often left the camp with as many pamphlets as he'd arrived with.

Arni Leino liked Brewster but was scared of him too. He'd heard enough stories to know the politics of labor could be bloody, and that the steepest costs were not always borne by professional men like Brewster and those who shouted on public corners. Arni had an uncle on his mother's side who'd gone to New York and said the wrong things in the wrong bar and finished the night with two broken legs. The Oregon coast wasn't that much different, and Arni figured the best way to keep his nose above water—and his sister's nose from sinking any deeper—was to skate somewhere along the line between politics. "A coward's winding route to hell" is what Brewster called it, but at least it was a path.

The U.S. Army came to Olney in the summer of 1917. Rather than Europe, some of the stoutest soldiers were sent to the Oregon coast to make sure the spruce would get cut for their military airplanes. The wood, smooth and light, didn't splinter and was plentiful in the great, rain-soaked forests of Clatsop and Tillamook counties. Reliable production, though, relied on a workforce that would do what was needed without strikes and other distractions.

First the army kicked out anyone who'd been seen talking with Brewster or any other Wob, then they set on the foreigners, especially any who had been sniffed out as a Red. The Finns got the toughest scrutiny, of course. Arni's friends Miko and Niklas, both as deliberately apolitical as he was, were pushed out of the camp, but Arni, for whatever reason, was allowed to stay. Perhaps because he'd been around longer, or perhaps because he sometimes did the work of two men with minimal complaint.

The oldest Finn at the camp, a man named Vilho, warned Arni that there'd be more purges. The war was intensifying, and the army would rather have soldiers in the woods guaranteeing their supply of spruce, cutting it themselves if they had to, rather than risk it with a bunch of revolutionaries loyal to some nonsense ideals that had nothing to do with winning in Europe.

"If you want to stay, change your name," Vilho told Arni. "Something American."

So Arni hastily filled out a few forms and took them to the county courthouse in Astoria. No one asked questions, and no one seemed to care. Old faces at camp kept calling him Arni, but as the months and years passed and new faces arrived, he became John G. Smith to most everyone.

Part 3 *Heat*

Chapter 14

1922

H. H. Flemming almost broke her leg the day after she met the men from the *Toveri* on the boat in mid-December 1922. They had pointed her in two directions: Chinatown and the offices of *The Western American*, the Ku Klux Klan's newspaper. She raised an eyebrow at both possibilities.

The *Toveri*'s editor shrugged. "We hear a lot of innuendos and rumors," he said, just before they climbed over the railing of the *Marie* and onto the docks.

"Can they be trusted?" Flemming asked.

"Can any of us?"

The next morning, in a cold drizzle, she set out for the Klan's newspaper offices in a former salmon cannery above the river. As she passed through downtown, she picked her way across the network of boards that spanned the burned-out pits of what had been, until a week prior, Astoria's busy city blocks. At Ninth and Commercial, one of the boards underfoot split with a dull crunch, and Flemming fell ten feet into a pile of ash, debris, blackened brick, and the spent remains of a fire hose, which broke her fall enough to keep any bones from shattering.

"Oh, for fuck!" she yelled as the rain piled on top of her.

"For fuck what?" came a man's thin voice a few long seconds later from up on the street level.

"For fuck's sake," Flemming clarified in a quieter tone. "That's what I meant to say. For fuck's sake. I fell down here."

"I know. I saw," the voice said, and a police officer's moony, smiling face peered over the edge of the pit. "Are you hurt, Inspector Flemming?"

It took several tries to stand up in the burned rubble, which shifted each time she tried to straighten up. Once she was on her feet, she was confused to find long strands of twisted silver and black tinsel all over her coat, wool pants, and boots.

"Owl Drug. That's what this used to be," the officer explained. "The whole thing was done up in Christmas decorations just a few nights before the fire."

"Charming."

"I'm Officer Wardle, by the way."

Flemming made her way to the side of the collapsed block and looked up. "Can you help me out of this godforsaken hole, Officer Wardle?"

Back up on street level, Wardle dusted off Flemming's back and picked away a few pieces of tinsel. She was a little embarrassed at the grooming but still dazed from the fall.

"Do you mind if I ask how the investigation is going?"

Flemming, still irritated by the fall, worked out a kink in her neck. "Well, it's not really much of an investigation at this point, Officer Wardle. I know there's been a fire; I know we've got an unholy mess on our hands; and I know that someone started it at Thiel's, for some reason, at some point in time. Probably with kerosene."

The cop was young, red-haired, and seemed happy to have the conversation.

"Does your mother know that you're out playing a policeman?" Flemming asked. "And how did you know my name?"

Wardle stiffened a bit. "I'm a beat cop. It's my job to know what's going on. I've been patrolling every inch of downtown since the fire. Have fought off my share of looters too." He pulled up a pant leg to reveal a purple and green bruise on his shin. "One of them bastards didn't care for my request to leave well enough alone. That's about the size of a wooden oar handle, don't you think?"

Flemming bent down to examine it, but Wardle dropped his pants over the wound before she could get a closer look. "And you can ask my mom your question when you get to the ever-after. Pneumonia. A year ago, September."

"I'm sorry. I was just poking fun."

His face softened. "I know. You alright? That was quite a fall."

Flemming told the officer she was headed toward the cannery where *The Western American* had its office. Wardle escorted her through town with a running commentary as they passed soldiers guarding charred bank vaults, the wrecked Stutz fire engine that had fallen into one of the chambers beneath town, and the ruins of the lawyer's office where, on the night of the fire, a man had leaped out of a second-story window onto a bedspread from the Weinhard Hotel held between three men.

"Do you know this Becker fellow?" Flemming asked.

Wardle let out a small laugh. "We know him. He's had folks riled up on all manner of—well, you name it, and he's probably had his stick stirring the piss pot, if you'll pardon the expression."

"Why would anyone pardon such an evocative description?" Flemming stopped walking. "Any idea why some Finns said I should talk to him about this fire?"

Wardle shrugged but said nothing. A few minutes later Flemming left him on the street and climbed the cannery stairs to knock on the door to the office of *The Western American*. The door fell open on its own, revealing Lem Becker standing alone with his arms folded, looking out at the river. The view was obscured by a cascade of rain droplets streaming down the window.

"Twice in two days. What a pleasure!" Becker smiled, motioning Flemming inside. "Come in and brighten up this place."

The pain from her fall was kicking in as her knees, hips, and back protested the next few steps into the office. She winced a little but didn't let on.

"Not every woman appreciates hearing this, but I must say you look like you've fallen off a truck," Becker said.

"Close enough," Flemming responded, dusting more of the ash and Christmas decorations off her coat. "Part of the job. So this is the hive of the empire?"

"The very same," Becker said with a half-mocking wave of his arm around the small room. "Say, we could use a woman of your capabilities and stature in our ranks. Our women's auxiliary does some of the most fruitful community service work in the entire organization. You ought to give it some consideration."

"Oh, I can't imagine that my lineage or my behavior would be all that endearing to your kind."

"Our kind? We are a big tent that welcomes many walks of life. Many indeed. And a woman as handsome as yourself—I can't imagine that you wouldn't qualify."

Flemming bristled. She shifted her weight to ease the pain in her knees, then worked her way around to the only chair in the office, the one behind Becker's desk that was scattered with stale issues of *The Western American*.

"By all means, make yourself at home," Becker said smugly.

Flemming suddenly noticed a stench hanging heavy in the room. "What the hell is that smell?"

Becker lit into a smile. "Well, you'll enjoy this: It seems one of the local fauna here, a seal I believe, became trapped in the pilings and burned up in the fire. I gather that some joker has wedged it beneath the floorboards somewhere in this building, just below this office, so that I could enjoy the process of its decomposition."

"A fan of your work here?" Flemming asked, opening the drawers of Becker's desk and digging through piles of papers.

"Can I help you find something?"

"Not sure. Have anything to sip on?"

Becker shooed Flemming's hands away from the desk and closed the drawers.

"Your kind of thirst won't get quenched here," Becker said. "You know that."

Flemming feigned disappointment. "Of course. I just thought a taste would help get that smell of rotting flesh out of my nose. Who did that anyway?"

Becker sighed. "This city is full of all manner of miscreants. And deeds have a way of eliciting—"

Flemming suddenly leaned back in the chair and tilted her head up at him. "Did you start this fire?"

"That's a horrible thing to say," Becker said.

"I know," Flemming said with a half-laugh. "It really is."

Becker strode across the room to look out the window again, putting his back to Flemming.

"You wouldn't be alone in the history of mankind in starting a fire," she continued. "And what if I told you I had it on good authority that one of your men was seen at the fire right after it started?"

"I'd say I'd like to know more about who that authority might be, because he's quite mistaken," Becker said. "And who are my men, anyway?"

Flemming took a long pause and pressed on. "You know, it's a funny thing to be charged with trying to understand how these kinds of things happen. So many of them have a way of starting and no one ever seems to know why. Like it's magic or something."

"I've never believed in magic. There was a good deal of coal underneath the Bee Hive is how I understand it, right next to the boiler," Becker said. "Coal is known to be flammable."

"You've heard about that? The Bee Hive and Thiel's Pool Hall? The basement below?"

"I do read the papers, if that's what you're asking."

A cargo ship on the river let go with a noisy blast of its horn. Flemming labored out of the chair and sidled up next to Becker at the big window to drink in the view of the rain-dimpled Columbia.

"I'll be unhappy if I have to come back and go over all this again," Flemming said. "Suppose we just get it over with now. Fill me in on how this whole mess happened. An accident, perhaps. A little revenge job that got out of hand. A murderous plot to destroy an entire town. Any of those will do."

"Will they?" Becker chuckled. "Certainly, Inspector Flemming. I'll be sure to pass along any relevant information should I ever come to possess it."

Flemming started toward the door. "On behalf of the Oregon State Fire Marshal's Office, we'd like to say in advance that we appreciate your cooperation in this matter. And I would note that withholding information, obstructing an investigation, might also be considered a crime."

Becker huffed. "Impertinent."

"Indeed it is," Flemming said over her shoulder.

As the door closed, she heard Becker ask, "Are you sure you know what you're doing?" She couldn't say that she was.

Chapter 15

1921

A year before the fire, in the fall of 1921, Lem Becker came to the Portland office of the Ku Klux Klan for the first time. It was barely an office at all.

"Every empire begins with nothing but an idea," Fred Giffords said when he noticed Becker's unimpressed expression on entering the back room of Hale's Mercantile off Burnside. Klan papers were mixed on a table with bags of flour and coffee, and a cat had to be shooed off a chair so Becker could sit. "But I'll take a room full of ideas any day over some empty furniture and emptier heads."

Giffords was short and rumpled with a gimpy left arm and a powerful voice. For years he'd been a line superintendent at Northwestern Electric and a faithful member of the Portland klavern, the Klan's local organization. Atlanta had just appointed him grand dragon for all of Oregon—$600 a month to make the state a powerhouse in the pursuit of 100 percent Americanism.

"HQ said you were a newspaperman ready to build the western realm," Giffords started in. "God knows we need every field sergeant we can get. We've got soldiers but not nearly enough leaders. The result, sad to say, is good intentions gone nowhere—'spilling your seed on the ground' as the Bible might say."

Just then a dark-haired woman in her mid-thirties walked into the back room, wincing at the last phrase and knitting her brows over her eyes. Becker watched as she wordlessly crossed the room to a shelf of canned green beans. She was handsome, fit, and seemed incongruent with a toady man like Giffords.

"Miss Darcy, we're having a meeting in here," Giffords said, a little upset by the intrusion.

She smiled, a little pained herself.

"I see that, Mr. Giffords," she said while she gathered an armful of cans. "Very important business, I'm sure. Saving the world from the likes of us." She made the sign of the cross with her free hand.

Giffords sighed and explained to Becker, "When the mercantile allows, Darcy answers our phones and occasionally takes over some of our administrative duties."

"Cash is cash," she addressed Becker directly. "It never goes as far as you want, so it never hurts to have a little more around."

"A universal truth," Becker responded.

"Even if, say, you are *despised* in some corners of the world. You still take what you can."

Giffords's face flushed a little. "Miss Darcy's Rome is infallible, she is sure of it, and we certainly part ways on that score."

"Heaven help us from ourselves," she said, shifting some of the cans so she could make a sign of the cross before she laughed and left the two alone again.

Becker had been a military propagandist during the war—stationed in London, Paris, and Siberia for a time—and then a newspaperman back home in Tennessee. The Klan, reignited after years of quiescence, had recruited him, knowing his father had been a full-blown member before he'd been temporarily ferried off to Canada after a Jewish lumber mill manager was shot and killed during what the Klan called a "house call." The local outfit had invited Becker to a private screening of *Birth of a Nation* in Pulaski, Tennessee, as part of an organized recruiting push and the promotion of a new sort of patriotism.

Growing up, Becker fancied himself more of a clever thinker than a fighter, so he'd never been particularly stirred by the Klan's frothing vitriol and late-night raids. More often than not, his father returned home from meetings smelling of liquor with his white sheet bundled under one arm. His eyes, heavy-lidded from the booze, hardly seemed to notice his wife or son unless the dishes were undone in the sink or his dinner wasn't heating on the stove. Those times, his rage erupted, and someone was bound to take a lashing.

In more sober moments, Becker's father tried to impart a tangled logic of grievances carried by the Klansmen against a roving cast of offenders. When pressed for details, his father resorted to a common refrain: "I don't care if you're dark-skinned, hook-nosed, rabbit-eared, or pope-infested, no one's taking what I got without a fight. Cowards don't live in this house." Becker never found out what his father's role was in the shooting at the lumber mill, only that he'd been somehow involved and that he'd come home with a lot of blood on his clothes. He hugged his family the next night and disappeared up north for almost a year. When he came back he was thinner and more bitter than before, more apt to pounce at the slightest provocation. He died of a heart attack within a few weeks, a day before Becker's sixteenth birthday.

That all happened as a young man. As an adult, when the recruiters came calling, something connected with the memory of his father, of protecting the family and eschewing cowardice. Plus there was new blood in the Klan now: men in suits with money and savvy. They understood that words, weaponized and ordered in the proper way, could be every bit as effective as blind violence, perhaps even more so. Becker developed a facility for language and had experienced its power during the war and then at home writing editorials for the newspaper. Over the course of a few weeks, the recruiter closed the deal with Becker with a combination of romantic notions of carrying on his father's legacy and tripling the meager salary he was making at the paper. He reported for duty at the Atlanta headquarters and, a week later, was shipped off to Oregon.

In the back room at Hale's, Giffords carried on about the pope and schools and false prophets. Becker nodded but his mind stayed on Darcy. She reminded him of a sharp-eyed, prickly woman he'd known in Russia who seemed to have a bottomless appetite for vodka but never managed to show any signs of the magnitude of drunkenness concomitant to the amount she drank. She was the person Becker always thought of when someone mentioned a woman who had "poise."

"Give men an enemy and, at first, most will cluster like sheep when wolves are on the hunt. But soon enough those sheep are a force unto their own and they start fighting back," Giffords said, pausing to stare at

Becker. "We've got Catholics, foreigners, boozers, Wobblies, socialists—it's a list as long as your mother's arm. The wolves are at the door, Mr. Becker, and this country is on the verge of becoming something you don't want to imagine."

It was a familiar grievance going back to Becker's childhood. Men like his father—and now Giffords—seemed to tap easily into a venom that Becker sometimes found hard to summon. Always something personal paired with the specter of America's foundation crumbling beneath their feet. Truth be told, Becker had to admit to himself, he'd been more intrigued by the remuneration he'd been promised along with the chance to be a mover and a shaker, someone with influence over the day's events. If that was the Klan's 100 percent Americanism, so be it. He was careful to not tip his hand as Giffords barreled on.

"Our people are in La Grande, Pendleton, Jacksonville, Eugene, even Tillamook," the grand dragon said. "But they need a voice, one that speaks for all of them, an echo chamber that reaffirms those already in our ranks and appeals to those on the fence. I need a newspaper, Mr. Becker, that provides us with fresh oxygen every single day. We have to feed their hearts and nourish their minds, give them something to live for when they wake up in the morning and to dream about when they go to bed at night. Can you do that, Mr. Becker?"

Becker set up the offices of *The Western American* a few months later on the top floor of a cavernous, defunct salmon cannery in Astoria, perched on timber pilings like a resting cormorant over the dull, green Columbia. *The Morning Astorian* had been there once, the landlord told him, back when the only toilet in the building was a hole cut in the floor above the river.

"Sea lions and salmon didn't seem to mind, but I'm told on a cold day that wind could blow all the way up into your throat," the man said.

Mercy, if the whole place wasn't gray. Most days, Becker found, the sky and the river were the same smudged and depthless color, interrupted by shades of green or brown. Siberia had been monochromatic, but it had nothing on Astoria. Becker challenged himself one afternoon to capture on paper how this place looked and felt but came up empty, only sure that it was heavy and oppressive and determined to swallow up anyone not anchored to the ground.

Atlanta had wired money and mailed him bundles of pamphlets, booklets, and even a letter from the imperial wizard himself, the national boss, congratulating him on embarking on the Klan's westward expansion and likening him to Coronado and his "spirit of conquest and enlightenment."

The first issue of *The Western American* didn't amount to much, just four broadsheet pages with recycled copy from Klan papers back East, screeds that lashed out at the Vatican, mysterious foreign plotters, and all forms of vice. Becker knew the pieces were poorly written and poorly argued, but they would do for now. Beneath the masthead he added "The Official Paper of the Invisible Empire, Knights of the Ku Klux Klan in the Realm of Oregon."

Becker quickly learned that Astoria was on its heels and bitterly so. Wages and production had been cut at the salmon canneries, the lumber mill, both flour mills, and even the cranberry canning shops. Pay dried up and any remaining dollars inevitably found their way toward temptation. Over on Taylor Street, booze was poured behind almost every closed door, and like a set clock, the Finns fought at the end of each night, sometimes for good reason, often for no other reason than to exercise primitive muscles gone lacking with the dwindling of good work. There were robberies, fires, stabbings, petty burglaries, and brazen holdups. Nighttime rain could just as easily be broken by thunder as it could the agonized cry of some victim downtown. Options dwindled, resentments swelled, and desperation took hold.

"Every crisis and opportunity needs a fulcrum, Mr. Becker," Giffords said during a visit. "Something that can be used to apply pressure, exert leverage, and produce results. Your new city has them in spades. None better, in my opinion, than demon alcohol."

There had been a rash of arrests and controversy over the city's booze business. The police raids were half-hearted and typically so well-forecasted that the proprietors had several hours to clean up their operations before the door was kicked open. Most in town liked it that way—the underground marketplace kept the city's economy humming on many days, and boozing gave them the wherewithal to continue on during these tough times. It also galvanized Astoria's most moralistic citizens.

Giffords seized the moment, wiring money to Becker with detailed instructions for the creation of the Astoria Law Enforcement League. "This must appear absolutely outside the clutches of the Invisible Empire and instead make a show of a growing movement of many: Protestants, Catholics, the chamber of commerce, the temperance societies—they all can have a seat at this table," Giffords added at the end of his instructions. "This will be a powerful allying force for our work. Let's birth a beast knowing that we may need to behead it at some opportune moment."

Reverend Wise at the First Methodist Church was the recipient of Giffords's seed money. Becker had learned the church's offertory plates, already meager with the economy, had been pilfered several times in recent weeks. Becker figured it was the reverend's doing, given the expensive tastes Mrs. Wise showed off around town, but he kept that to himself. Becker went to the church on a Monday morning, entering through the back door to find the reverend at his desk staring out the window toward the river. Becker explained the arrangement, handed over $300 in cash, and was utterly candid about the Klan's goals and the need for secrecy.

The reverend grinned. "Even miracles come with conditions," he said.

With the temperance movement freshly seeded and watered, Giffords soon turned his attention to growing the ranks of the Invisible Empire. Becker, always a numbers man, had been looking at the newest census figures. He'd brought them to Portland, partially in hopes of seeing Miss Darcy again, but she wasn't in that day.

"Did you know that six in ten in Astoria have a foreign-born parent? I saw a story about it in the paper," he asked Giffords. "We are awash, of course, in Finns, but there are Swedes and Chinese and Japanese and Russians; the list goes on."

"Yes, yes, and nine out of ten in the Klan's other realms in this great state—I'm thinking of places like La Grande and Eugene and even Tillamook—are U.S. citizens through and through. So why are we in

Astoria when there are so many foreign-borns here? Is that your question, Mr. Becker, perhaps that we'd do better to shore up other places where the odds are more amply stacked in our favor?"

"Yes, that's precisely my question."

"Precisely because of that very fact. Astoria is on the front lines, and this is where the fight will be won or lost. There's low-hanging fruit to be picked in Pendleton and Gresham and Roseburg, but this is the place where the invisible army, should we build it, will generate the greatest strength because it will overcome the greatest obstacles," Giffords said. "Mr. Becker, we are at a very pregnant point in our country's history. If we are not careful and do not move strongly and swiftly, we are destined to become strangers in the very land our fathers gave us."

The little man had a dangerous, dim view of the world, Becker thought, but perhaps he was onto something.

"And think about it another way, Mr. Becker—in a geological way. Here we are at the edge of our continent, buffeted by the winds and currents and waves of an ocean whose endless tides deliver invaders of every stripe and have for long before you and I arrived . . ."

"The Chinooks and the Clatsops wouldn't argue with you on that score."

"Don't get smart. We are keepers of the gate here at the mouth of this great river and this great country. Every American from this spot eastward relies on the guardians of this gate whether they know it or not. You'd be wise to take your responsibility seriously."

"Oh, I do," Becker responded. He made a show of unfolding a piece of paper from his back pocket. "Now I just want to be sure I understand the structure of the army we're fielding. The fine people who will be a bulwark against sin and debauchery."

Giffords gave him a deadpan look that Becker ignored.

"The lexicon is what I'm learning here, so bear with me," he continued, focusing on his paper. "You're the, ah, the head dragon of the operation. I've got that down. Then we've got your 'grand goblins,' and those are the state recruiters and they've got their local operators called 'kleagles,' if I've got that right. Now for every man they pull into our outfit, each of the kleagles gets four dollars. Makes sense to me; give a man a job to do and pay him for it."

Giffords nodded slowly.

"But how to cover those costs? That initiation fee, of course, for every new man who comes aboard. Now that's called the, ah . . ." Becker ran his finger down the paper, "that initiation fee is the 'klecktoken.' Have I got that right? And then there's a 'king kleagle' who is the boss of the 'grand goblin.' Do I have a bead on that?"

"If you're trying to amuse yourself here, Mr. Becker, I'd suggest you tread lightly. The empire is the most savage to those who turn against them."

"Violence?"

"Whatever it takes to scrub away the filth."

Becker grew more serious and put his paper away. Giffords seemed pleased.

"The churn of the pot is what makes every meal a success," Giffords said, picking up again. "We can't and we won't sit still in this business, Mr. Becker. Every man who enters our ranks can bring with him another ten men that he knows. And each of those can bring ten more and so forth and so on. When you pay a kleagle, you're investing in a system that can sustain itself through vigorous growth."

"But there is an end to it finally, is there not? At some point, there are no more men to recruit and no minds left to correct. Who is left footing the bill then?"

Giffords smiled broadly and whacked Becker's shoulder with a rolled-up copy of the paper. "My friend, we should be so lucky to ever have that kind of trouble."

The Klan made its first public appearance in Astoria at the First Methodist Church downtown in February 1922. The Astoria Law Enforcement League had spent an hour railing against the speakeasies and shouting rumors about which cops were on the take and which city council members were only too happy to look the other way as the city degenerated into rank sin. Just as they began to pass an offertory plate, the doors swung open at the back of the church and three men in white hoods and robes entered and walked in melodramatic silence up the aisle. The first Klansman held a twenty dollar bill high over his head and deposited it on the altar and then all three turned and left wordlessly the way they'd come in.

Becker, who'd arranged it all, had positioned himself in the back row of the church. He stifled a chuckle as the shortest of the trio stumbled over his robe as they left. The show made the front page of *The Morning Astorian* the next day.

Chapter 16

1922

Astoria's Klan, properly seeded and fed, grew at a staggering rate. Lem Becker marveled as recruitment hit the sweet spot. No longer was he solely relying on a small army of loyal kleagles. Now the ranks swelled as neighbors enlisted neighbors, churches extolled the Klan's virtues on Sunday mornings, and strangers knocked on his door unsolicited, hoping to get a story idea placed in the columns of *The Western American*. Becker learned that his paper drew the best response when he sprinkled his text with bits of paranoia and resentment alongside a dash of puffed-up patriotism. It became essential reading for those intrigued by the idea of "100 percent Americanism."

A few dozen local Klansmen became a hundred by the spring, several hundred by the middle of the summer, and nearly a thousand as the leaves began to change colors. The twice-monthly meetings had to be moved from Becker's newspaper office to the basement of the Methodist church. Across the state the Klan made its presence known: crosses burned dramatically on Portland's Mount Tabor and in the city square at La Grande, more than one thousand men in robes marched through the streets of Ashland in the middle of the day, and Tillamook's quiet streets suddenly became a dangerous place for unfamiliar faces or those speaking a foreign tongue.

"We've got fourteen thousand members in fifty-eight klaverns," Giffords bragged. "That's an army by any way you imagine it."

Astoria's klavern took some work to organize, especially with such a large group. A car salesman named Hawkins was put in charge. He was followed by the kligrapp, the kludd, the klabee, the klexter, and a series of couriers and messengers called nighthawks. Each position was filled by men who'd undergone initiation rites, men who were bankers, dockworkers, fishermen, hardware store owners, police officers, railroaders, teachers—all manner of citizens, so long as they weren't Catholic, foreign, or a color other than white.

Hawkins and Becker agitated the Klan's enemies, holding events and tirelessly railing in the columns of *The Western American*. The Klan hosted an event at the city auditorium one night, seating a dozen hooded men in a semicircle on stage around a cross that burned loudly, hissing as the flames scorched the sap. Hundreds sat silently in the audience, some in hoods, others in street clothes.

"The Roman Catholic Church is alien in its government, heretical in its teachings, and tyrannical and despotic in its practices," one of the cloaked men said, raising his voice above the din. "It claims both spiritual and temporal sovereignty over the souls of men through the exercise of political and ecclesiastical power by the pope. We know that is a lie, and we know that is what we must unite against."

On another night, Becker arranged for a lecture by Sister Lucretia, a former nun who had been a nurse at Portland's St. Vincent Hospital but had left the church for its "insidious godlessness." Becker also paid two actors from Seattle to join the presentation as former priests of the Catholic Church who now denounced its desire to corrupt the youngest of minds. The event turned into a near-riot when a member of the audience stood up to defend the church and was mobbed by four men, one of whom punched the man in the ear with a roll of pipe inside his fist. "The pope sends a single man to speak up for his vile institution against a show of strength like this?" the emcee quipped after the dazed and bloody man had been dragged outside. "That itself is evidence enough of his folly."

The Klan made a showing of benevolence in Astoria. At one point, men in robes entered a meeting of the Women's Christian Temperance Union to donate eighty dollars in cash. Attached was a note stating that the money was intended to support the construction of a children's home.

It read: "Be assured that we may be relied upon at all times to support, in every way possible, the great work you are pursuing."

Becker made sure that Reverend Wise found his way into *The Morning Astorian*'s story on the dramatic donation.

"I can merely say that I hold the Klansmen deep in my heart," Wise said, "and that I am proud that these men have proven themselves to be organized to perpetuate true Americanism and the higher ideals. Their aim is indeed a modern crusade of righteousness and mercy, and my praise of that aim is unstinted."

Meanwhile Becker and his Klansmen were relentless in applying pressure to business leaders with a careful conflation of politics: if you didn't stand with the Klan, you were standing with everyone else, including the narcotics pushers, the booze sellers, the very agents of sin ripping at the fabric of Astoria's civility. There was no third way. Those who refused to join were publicly shamed, maligned in *The Western American*, and boycotted not only by the Klan's growing ranks but by their families as well.

Within months the Finnish foreman was fired from the Union Salmon Cannery, Catholic members were forced from the school board, and an Irish Catholic named O'Brien, the popular head of the Astoria Chamber of Commerce, was disgusted to suddenly find himself out of a job. A Greek immigrant named Hull fled town after *The Western American* ran a front-page story that claimed he was selling beer out of his barber shop and skimping on his rent.

"If you love the good old U.S. of A., find this fiend Hull and bring him a dose of justice," Becker wrote. "That goes for any member of the alien forces of evil responsible for so many of our ills today."

Becker also campaigned tirelessly against the Knights of Columbus, the Catholic Church's fraternal organization. He printed pamphlets with insinuations of incest, corruption, and debauchery and distributed them liberally around town. One night in June, as the Knights adjourned one of their meetings, they were met with about fifty hooded Klansmen outside their building, some holding torches. An angry standoff ensued and Leb Karlsson, the city's police chief, soon found himself between both groups, holding each at bay with stiffened arms.

"There'll be no bloodshed here tonight!" he shouted. "Unless, of course, you'd rather spend tonight in jail instead of your beds at home."

Becker stepped up to the police chief. He never wore the hood and robe.

"It would seem a shame to arrest some of your very own sergeants and patrol officers," Becker said in a low voice, motioning with his chin to the restless Klansmen. "Citizens of our city expect policemen to be on their beat, not idling in some jail cell."

"I don't give two bits about who gets arrested," the police chief said, raising his voice for everyone to hear. "Whether you're one of my men or you clean the shitters at the mill, if you're making trouble tonight, plan to spend the night together in a cell. Now get the hell out of here."

Becker opened his mouth to respond to Karlsson, but the police chief stepped into the crowd and pulled the hood off a man to reveal a doughy insurance agent.

"Jesus Christ, Dan Perkins?" Karlsson sneered. "This is where you've cast your lot?"

The insurance agent looked dumbfounded and vulnerable. From somewhere in the crowd, a Klansman said loudly, "Someone's got to protect this town, chief. And if it isn't you, it's us."

Karlsson grabbed the hoods off more men, bug-eyed brothers who worked on the railroad. He swiped at a few more, but the Klansmen began an uneasy retreat. "Who else is here?" the chief demanded.

The Knights of Columbus stepped forward as the Klan moved back. The chief halted their progress with both arms.

"And you're not much better, except at least you have the courage not to hide behind a borrowed pillowcase," Karlsson said. "Everyone go home and spend the night with your wives or girlfriends or whatever you find company in. I don't care, just get off my streets."

Becker stood aside as both groups finally dispersed. He found Karlsson as he walked back toward his car.

"Uneasy times, I'm afraid, chief," he said. "I respect that it's your job to preserve law and order, but there's no denying there's an ill wind blowing."

Karlsson didn't answer and didn't bother to turn to Becker, instead choosing just a single finger to say goodnight.

Chapter 17

1922

Aside from the Klan, the men from the *Toveri* had pointed H. H. Flemming toward Chinatown. The rumor was that the fire was connected with the killing of a man named Go Yet six months before, sometime in the spring of 1922. Flemming didn't care for that theory because it seemed too far-fetched—*who would burn down the city to hide a body when it would've been all too easy to drop it into the river or truck it deep into the woods and let the forest and ferns swallow it whole?* Still the Go Yet connection seemed plausible to Paulo, the Finn radical she'd met with on the boat, just so long as the rumor's origin didn't find its way back to him or anyone else at the *Toveri*. "We already have trouble to spare," he had said.

She searched out Wardle a few days after her visit with Lem Becker in the offices of *The Western American*. Chinatown was sometimes part of Wardle's walking beat, she remembered, and he might have something on the rumor from the *Toveri* boys. She found him on Commercial Street, hunching his shoulders against the rain at the doorway of a burned-out tannery, not looking particularly busy. He reminded her of a wet dog unsure of whether to shake or just be miserable in the cold.

"How do, inspector," he said. "Hope this weather suits you better than it does me."

"Suits me fine," she said lightly, hands deep in her pockets. "I'd hope a policeman might not be too deterred by a little sprinkle. Certainly wouldn't bode well if some trouble worse than inclement weather suddenly cropped up."

Wardle twitched with a bit of shame.

"Do you know I was held up right over there?" Wardle said, pointing over his left shoulder. "Two days after the fire, I was watching over a couple of safes from the Bank of Astoria, all melted shut and whatnot. This was before the army showed up. This ugly little man first tries to bribe me, says he'll give me five dollars for ten minutes alone with the safe. I refused, of course, and then he chased me off with a gun, one of those snubby ones that fit in your pocket."

Flemming couldn't help but laugh. "I thought you were a policeman. You can't run off like that. Isn't there some kind of vow you take not to turn your back on trouble?"

"The only vow I've taken is not to come home all shot full of holes. Let them have whatever the bank keeps in that foolin' safe."

"Well, the city's lucky to have such a brave soul in its ranks," Flemming deadpanned. Before he could answer, she ran the Go Yet rumor past him. Wardle was familiar since he was one of the first on the scene and had testified during the coroner's inquest. The man had been shot in the hallway of a boarding house as he came out of the toilet, hit in the chest, thigh, and once in the spot where the bottom of his nose joined his face.

"Fatal blow," Wardle said, tapping the same place under his nose.

"Motive?"

"Sideways with the wrong people, best I could tell," Wardle said. "Maybe owed someone money. Maybe tried to cut into someone else's business. We didn't get very close to the bottom of it."

Wardle said that the week after Go Yet was shot, the naked body of a man named Po was found in a heap on Astor Street. His back had been broken and his nose was gone. He'd been taken to the roof of the Louvre, the three-story bar, restaurant, and roller rink on Commercial where he was stripped down, bloodied up, and tossed over the side.

"Some kind of retribution," Flemming shrugged. "And what does this have to do with the fire?"

Wardle stomped his feet against the cold as the rain dripped onto his face. "Search me."

Flemming liked Chinatown and was happy to have an excuse to go. It was bigger a few years back, tucked into the swampier side of downtown, but the latest bitter wave of anti-Chinese sentiment—enforced by violence, low pay, and boycotts—had driven hundreds out of town, including families that had done the most difficult work in the canneries for decades. Now, even though it was just a couple of blocks long, it still felt like its own world, with the smell of steaming noodles and urgent murmurs of foreign voices coming from behind closed doors.

The only woman Flemming really knew in Chinatown was Shu Fong. She owned a small market that had burned down a few years back. She'd done a poor job covering her tracks—only amateurs used gasoline—but Flemming classified it as accidental. She needed the insurance money since the cannery owners had cut wages when the spring salmon runs didn't materialize.

Her new shop survived the downtown fire and now bustled with people in ash-covered coats looking to stock up on supplies. Flemming found Shu Fong in the back of the store.

"Did you know this man, Go Yet? The one who was shot?" Flemming asked after reintroducing herself. "What about the other man tossed off the roof? Was it the tongs?"

She straightened up, rubbed her hands on her apron, and maintained her silence.

Flemming sighed. "I could use some help here."

"Why don't you talk a little louder so they can hear you all the way down to Warrenton?"

The investigator recalled that Shu Fong had a bit of an acid tongue, which she also remembered liking. She asked Flemming to return later that night after the shop closed. They ate soup at a table in the back room, and Shu Fong warmed up after being reminded of Flemming's favor.

"I can help, but you can't be in my store asking questions. And same with the policeman. I sell to everyone in town and can't afford to have you casting a shadow over my shop."

"Casting a shadow. That hurts just a little," Flemming said.

"A big shadow too," Fong quipped, giving Flemming an obvious once-over with her eyes.

"Ouch."

Fong claimed she didn't know who killed Go Yet but figured it had something to do with the tongs, the underground organizations that seemed to never be far from trouble.

"Who knows which one? Bo Sin Seer. On Yick. They all have their teeth in drinks or girls or card games . . . They come, they make trouble, fighting like petty children, and they leave. The rest of us, the people who live here, are left to sweep up the mess," she said. "It's not right."

Flemming nodded slowly.

"And if things go really wrong, they call in the Boo How Doy. You know this?" Shu Fong continued without waiting for an answer. "Every tong has hatchet men. When they visit, you either die or wish you had. I know the Swedes have a similar kind of man, same with the Irish—built like trees but mean. Is this really what they must do?"

Flemming had heard countless stories about these enforcers of all stripes, about a man whose nostrils were ripped in half, about two brother thieves bound together and dangled headfirst into the Columbia off the cannery pier till they drowned, about toes cut off the foot of some poor soul and mailed to his family. Maybe Go Yet had run afoul of the wrong person, and maybe the fire was somehow related? It didn't seem to quite fit, but Flemming didn't want to let it go until she'd probed a bit further. "Can you get me a name? That would be it; that'd be all I'd ask of you. Debt paid."

Flemming woke up two mornings later and found a scrap of paper that had been slipped beneath her door at the Elliott Hotel. It said "Bao Chen, Chee Kong tong. Find him at the Suomi sauna each morning."

Flemming was surprised to find the sauna open. Most businesses in Astoria were still closed because of the fire, but the sauna was less of a business and more of a cultural necessity to the Finns. It was where deals were brokered, gossip was exchanged, matches were made, and futures were decided—all among the pungent steam twisting lazily inside little wooden rooms.

She showed her badge to the man working the lobby just inside the front door. He was old and stout like a barrel, with a mop of blond hair that brushed into his eyes.

"I'm looking for a man, Mr. Chen, has he been in today?"

The man nodded.

"May I see him?" Flemming asked.

"Women this side," the man said, thumbing to a door over his left shoulder. "Twenty-five cents."

Flemming smiled. "Well, is Mr. Chen on that side?"

He shook his head. "Men this side," he said, thumbing over his right shoulder.

"Well, it's not going to do me much good to go on the women's side then, is it?"

"I think you'll find it very relaxing."

Flemming let out a long sigh, set her eyes on this man, this guardian of the sauna, and showed her badge again. She was a head taller than him and made sure he knew it, broadening her shoulders and lowering her voice. "I'm on official business on behalf of the state of Oregon. There are two very simple options here. You take me to see Mr. Chen right now or this business is reported to the commerce bureau for a long list of violations that I'm more than happy to swear to under oath."

The man gave her a dull, slow look from beneath his blond hair. "Twenty-five cents."

Paid up, Flemming was escorted through the men's side of the sauna, pausing every few steps in the hallway as the man from the front desk pulled open one wooden door after another, allowing a billowing pulse of steam to escape before poking his head inside. "No Mr. Chen," he said with each one. Finally, at the last door at the end of the hall, he nodded his head and opened the door, telling Flemming: "Mr. Chen."

Inside, she saw a small Chinese man, naked but for a white towel across his waist, hunched on a wooden bench as vapor swirled around him. He glanced at her with sleepy eyes but showed no signs of being shocked that a woman was standing there, much less a woman in a wool pants, thick coat, and dirty boots. He was hitting his back with a fistful of sticks in a slow, laborious rhythm.

The room smelled like juniper and sweet oils. The heat was thick and oppressive but also intoxicating. Flemming watched beads of steam appear on her coat and felt them soak into her face for several long moments as she listened to the man swat his back with the switches. As it became harder to breathe, she dug the badge out of her coat and held it up for him to see.

"Mr. Chen," she said finally, "I'm looking for information about Go Yet." The swats continued and the moisture streamed off Flemming's nose and into her lap. "The man who was shot this summer. He came out of the toilet and someone lit into him. Then another man was killed, in retaliation it seems. Thrown off the top of the Louvre."

Chen grunted, fell silent, and then said wearily, "I work in the cannery. Why would I know anything about that?"

The door opened and a rotund man, already slicked with sweat and wearing only a wet towel, took a step inside the sauna, then stopped short when he saw Flemming. Chen motioned the man out the door with his chin and the fellow complied without a word. After another long moment Chen rose and used a second towel to pick a metal bucket off the floor and began swishing its water. He smiled at Flemming, raising his eyebrows in a way that was friendlier than Flemming would've imagined from a man in the business of enforcement. "May I?"

Flemming smiled. "Of course," she said, hoping that he wouldn't.

He spilled the bucket's contents across the bed of baking rocks just inside the entrance. The rocks let out a loud, hissing sigh and filled the room with a fresh infusion of gauzy steam. Flemming released her own sigh as the man settled back onto the bench. *Is this man really a killer? A nostril-ripper?* It was hard to figure; his face seemed untouched by violence and his voice was silky and pleasant.

The investigator clarified, "I actually don't have much interest in Go Yet or how he died or why. I have a job, and that's to find out what started the fire the other night. My boss is the state fire marshal and his boss is the governor and the cause of this fire is of interest to both of them, I suspect. I would dearly like to fill out my report, tell them what they'd like to hear, and get back home." The sweat was now soaking Flemming's head, dripping into her eyes, and snaking down the ridge of her spine. She stripped off her coat and wiped her face with the inside lining. "There was a rumor that I'm checking on, that the fire was related to what happened to this man, Go Yet," she said, pausing for a few beats of the switch tapping on the man's back. "Know anything about that?"

The man turned his head to look at Flemming and swept a handful of wet hair away from his eyes. "We all have someone we have to answer to, don't we? It's the nature of things, so I'm sympathetic," Chen said. "I can tell you this, because I hear a lot of things around the cannery, of course: what happened to Mr. Yet, well, there's simply no relation to the terrible events of that fire."

Flemming nodded for a long time and let her body slouch under the heat, wondering how so many Finns could take a sauna so often and not turn to kelp. Mr. Chen sat still, and it was clear he had nothing more to say. When she got up to leave, the two shook hands like businessmen at the end of a negotiation, each with sort of an empty half-smile.

"A funny thing," Chen said and then stopped as if he was debating whether to go on. Flemming waited. "There used to be a flower store on Duane Street that I always went to when I first came to Astoria because they carried dried flowers that my daughter liked to use for tea. Jasmine and hibiscus. I would sometimes mail her a bundle. Very sad to lose that shop in the fire."

"Indeed," Flemming said with her hand on the sauna's door handle. "And the funny thing?"

"After it happened I was on the block where the flower shop used to be, paying my respects to the owner." He paused to clear the sweat from his face with a long swipe from top to bottom. "I ran into the dentist who pulled a tooth for me last spring." Another pause. "And we're talking, and this dentist tells me about being visited by someone who said he'd been the one who started the fire."

"And?"

"And then the rain was coming down, so that was it. We were all running along, going in our different directions," Chen said, blinking sweat from his eyes.

Flemming shook out of her vapor reverie.

"What's his name, the dentist?"

"It's not a him. It's a her."

Part 4 *Sparks*

Chapter 18

1922

In May 1922, seven months before the city burned, two cargo ships collided just inside the mouth of the Columbia River: the *S.S. Iowan*, inbound with timber from Tacoma, and the outgoing *Welsh Prince*, full of wheat from eastern Oregon. The *Iowan* escaped with little damage, but the *Welsh Prince* was badly wounded, and a fire in the hold killed seven men.

The crews of both ships were forced to stay in Astoria while the insurance agents tried to sort out how two ships could collide in a mile-wide river and who would get the bill. A stranded boatswain from the *Iowan* found his way to John Black's back room, eager to feast on cocaine packets but unable to pay in a way that matched his appetite. In the early morning gloom, the boatswain tried in vain to bargain with John Black for narcotics he'd already consumed, and the crewman found himself stabbed twice in the liver. He stumbled for several minutes through the empty blocks of downtown and died on the lawn of City Hall.

John Black made sure that the police found their way to Lily Leino's boardinghouse room, right to a bloody knife in the drawer of her bedside table.

Lily was arrested for the killing of the *Iowan* boatswain and was taken to the jail near the courthouse. She'd been in an opium fog when the man had been killed and struggled to account for her whereabouts. "Where do *you* tend to go when you're in that state?" she asked the investigator through a half-smile and glassy eyes.

The murder charge was mostly based on a sworn statement from John Black that he'd seen the two of them in a dispute earlier that night, first at a secret bar behind Stevenson's Restaurant and later on the street. Lily, Black attested, had been spurned by the man because of her despicable drug habit and had a "tendency to react violently when she's been shamed." That, along with the stained knife in her drawer, was enough for a police sergeant to arrest Lily. John Black was a well-known criminal and liar, but the whole of it would be up to the prosecutor to sort out.

Lily shared a jail cell with several of the girls from Bond Street, who looked more bored than frightened. But as she came out of her daze, a grim cloud settled around her. The next day her brother came to visit.

"Arni! What has happened?"

She was exasperated, frustrated, and full of tears. He didn't know what to say except that he was just as confused. The police investigator had told him what John Black had said about the dead boatswain and the knife, then shrugged.

"Is any of it true?" Arni asked his sister.

"None of it is true, I don't think. I would never stab someone, veli, and if I had, wouldn't I remember?"

When they were children, Lily had been the gentler of the two. As a young boy, Arni built traps to capture mice that had tunneled into their cupboards to dine on their bread. When the traps were a success, his plan had been to stuff them into a canvas bag with some rocks and toss them into the stream not far from their house. Lily begged him not to until he relented. Somewhere inside she was still that person, he suspected, but he hadn't seen her for some time.

Arni had Lily recite everything she remembered about that night, which wasn't much, and was relieved that their father and mother weren't around to see their daughter in such a terrible fix.

"None of what he said is true, Arni. It can't be." She choked up and grabbed his arm. He let her cry for a long moment.

"It can't be," he said, repeating it aloud to convince himself.

"If this is really happening to me, I can't . . . I won't survive this, Arni. I can't. You know me. I can't live in jail; I'm not a captive. It will crush me into nothing, God, like I never existed. But I exist; I do, Arni! I know it's been bad—I'm too deep into too many bad things—but you know that's not me. It's never been me."

He rubbed his face in the hopes of clearing his mind. "You're stronger than you think," he said and watched the light behind her eyes flicker a little brighter but only for a split second. "You turned a dark corner like a lot of us do . . ."

He remembered something she'd told him once about her sickness and her desperate need for the contents of John Black's packets. You woke up in the morning in a state of "almost-death," she'd said, and spent the rest of your day chasing the thing that gave you life, leaving you in a constant state of terror and exhaustion, doing whatever it took not to face that death and sickness again.

"The real me still exists," she insisted quietly. "You have to know that, Arni."

For a moment he considered correcting her. *I'm John Smith now; you know that, and that's what you should call me.* He'd told her before, but she always shook her head, refusing to concede to the change.

"Your name is who you are and where you come from," Lily had told him the first time he'd mentioned it. "It's like a traveler's trunk containing your whole life that you can never set down. No one can be allowed to erase your name, even you," she'd added with her hand on his arm. But here he was, being erased, one mishap and one small tragedy at a time. The same could be said for Lily, he realized. She'd been vanishing for years into this tumultuous life of hers, and now this mess with the murdered man threatened to finish the job.

He went straight from the jail to the furniture store where John Black's business operated from the back room. The front door was locked, so he sprinted around to the back, wondering what he planned to do when he got there. But the back door was locked too, and he banged on it until his arm ached. Before he left he smashed two windows with his elbow, hoping at the least that it might invite thieves to walk away with some of John Black's little paper packets.

Chapter 19

1922

In the same summer of 1922, not long after the *Iowan* and the *Welsh Prince* collided, a gray whale washed up on a beach near Hammond, a tiny beachside village south of Astoria. For weeks it drew regular crowds of the curious. The rotting stench rode the incoming breeze for everyone who approached it, but the whale was a magnificent and terrible sight. Parts of its flesh were already hacked away by a few adventurous eaters, and the rest was pinned onto the beach as if by the finger of God.

Lem Becker had been driving north from Seaside on a Sunday afternoon and heard about the whale when he stopped in Warrenton for coffee. He'd loved the story of Owen Chase, the ship *Essex*, and its calamitous run-in with the sperm whale in the South Pacific but had never seen a whale in person. By coincidence he arrived to find many of his fellow Klansmen there, out of their robes, of course, clustered together like chicks in the sand.

He slapped them on the shoulders and made small talk about the whale but then steered the conversation toward the previous night's news. Five young people had been drinking at the Whistle Stop in Flavel and left near midnight. A few minutes later their car slid off the road and into a band of towering trees. Three of them had died.

Becker recounted the story, even though it had been all over the morning paper, and then solemnly stared at each of the men in turn. "There are small moments in history, men, when painful events provide an impetus for transformation," he said. "Do you follow?"

The men were silent for a long moment until one of them, a clerk with the railroad, kicked the toe of his shoe through the sand and shook his head. "I don't believe we do."

"Opportunity." Becker sighed. "I'm talking about opportunity in the face of calamity. The tragedy of these young people whose lives were snuffed short so unceremoniously."

Becker's wheels turned faster as his cohorts seemed hopelessly stuck.

"We get the calamity part; that's clear as day, Lem. I'm afraid we're foggy on the rest until you explain yourself."

Instead Becker took one last walk around the leviathan on the beach, marched toward his car, and continued hatching a plan to himself.

Three nights after the fatal car wreck, Reverend Wise called an emergency meeting of the Astoria Law Enforcement League at the First Methodist Church. One of the people who attended was the father of a young woman from the Whistle Stop who'd been killed. Lem Becker had given him a ride and, so as not to be seen, dropped him a block away from the meeting.

"This has to end," the father pleaded as soon as the meeting came to order. He was standing in the center of a circle of two dozen dour men and women. "I have lost someone very, very dear to me, and I'll be damned if I'm going to let it happen to anyone else." Tears gathered on his face and worked their way into his beard. "We either fix this right or we quit talking."

After the meeting Becker found the reverend and delivered $100 in cash. He also had a letter he'd typed up with Reverend Wise's name at the bottom. "To the community, our long journey to temperance has been long and fraught, but this week we step into the breach and begin a course of correction and healing . . ."

The letter, published in *The Morning Astorian* a day later, explained distress over the incident at the Whistle Stop, noting that since it occurred outside the city limits, it was a matter for Sheriff Nelson. "We, the Astoria Law Enforcement League, have pleaded with Sheriff Nelson to clean up the Whistle Stop and other similar dens that pose a danger to our community. Because of insufficient action, we are now compelled to assert our own measures. We call on all concerned citizens to be at the Whistle Stop tomorrow night at seven, armed if able, to shut down this scourge on our community."

The Whistle Stop wasn't much: a squat windowless building just off the highway between Astoria and Warrenton in the hamlet of Flavel, a town named after a local sea captain who built a business around climbing aboard ships and navigating them across the treacherous Columbia River bar. The building had been a storage barn for the railroad, but recently it'd been converted into an illegal nightspot frequented by all manner of parched citizens, including local police. The beer and whiskey flowed freely and copiously, but the star attraction was a homemade billiards table constructed from the deck of a fishing boat called the *Missy Lou*.

More than fifty showed up that night at the Whistle Stop. By Becker's view, most of them had at least one gun. They weren't unruly, but they also didn't cooperate when Sheriff Nelson and his deputies stepped between the crowd and the front entrance to the Whistle Stop. Becker had called a meeting of the Klan that morning, just to be sure there'd be a crowd at the spectacle, and was pleased to see so many had showed up and brought some of their friends.

"Robes?" one of them had asked when the morning meeting was breaking up. "If so, I'll need to borrow someone's. I'm not sure where mine is."

"What? No. No robes, for Christ's sake," Becker fumed. "This is a different kind of show of force."

The newspapers were at the Whistle Stop too, and the reporters scribbled furiously as citizen after citizen stepped forward to address Sheriff Nelson.

"You either take your men in there and clean this place out or we do it for you," one of them finally said, lowering his rifle into the gut of the sheriff. Several others followed suit. "Either way, tonight is the last night the Whistle Stop serves illegal booze."

"We'll burn it down if we have to," another said. "Don't test us on that score."

Sheriff Nelson showed no sign of budging. He'd been in the liquor business since the second week after the prohibition vote. It was an open secret for anyone who cared to know, and often the money he made went to buy equipment for the department or give bonuses to his deputies, who had become deeply loyal to him. He pocketed some of the cash, of course, drank up his fair share, and often found something else to do when it came time for the local cops to crack down on bootleggers. It was, for Astoria, the kind of harmonious arrangement that seemed to benefit all—except this growing army of teetotalers now in front of him.

Just then the owner, a squat man with strands of silver hair that almost touched his shoulders, came out smiling with his hands in the air.

"Sorry folks, we're closed for the night!" he said, raising his arms even higher in mock terror. "Come back tomorrow if you're still thirsty!"

The mob began shouting and closing in on him, but he disappeared back inside.

"Fair enough, folks, you made your point loud and clear. Time for us to go back home to our families in one piece," Sheriff Nelson said.

Rain began to fall and the crowd eventually broke up, half-certain that they'd been victorious. Becker stayed around a while longer to make sure the reporters had all they needed for their front-page stories the next morning.

"Don't take my word on this, but what I believe you just saw was Astoria's finest finally banding together to take back this city," Becker said, speaking slowly enough so they could capture his words in their notebooks. "I saw judges in the crowd tonight, men of the cloth, even the head of the chamber of commerce. About the only person of note who wasn't doing his part to clean up this filth, I'm afraid, was Sheriff Nelson."

The armed standoff played big in the papers for several days and became the topic of conversation for a week. Accounts varied about how many people were there—Fifty? Five hundred? One thousand?— but the theme had been set about the profound failings of the Clatsop County sheriff. *Once you ring a bell*, Becker thought, *it cannot be unrung. And soon the echoes are all that you hear.*

A month later, at the end of July 1922, there was a special election. Becker worked feverishly to line up votes and curry favor with the Democratic and Republican parties in town. Arms were twisted, money was exchanged, newspaper editors were buttonholed, anonymous letters were left in mailboxes, and promises were made. By the end of the night, Sheriff Nelson was out and Sheriff Harley Slusher, a barely working mechanic who spoke of restoring laws and values of the righteous but quiet majority, was in. He spoke highly of the Klan and all it was doing for Astoria and its citizens.

Chapter 20

1922

Astoria was buzzing with electric tension in early October 1922. The new sheriff was cracking down on the bootleggers, the Hammond Mill had just burned on the Astoria docks, the ranks of Astoria's Ku Klux Klan had swelled to nearly nine hundred, and paranoia over the socialists, communists, and other Reds spread liked never before. Lem Becker, building on the victory of Sheriff Nelson's ouster, had assembled a group of Klansmen to run for city council and mayor, which lit the flame of a roiling war for Astoria's soul and future. On one side was the old guard, who tolerated, even fanned, the city's messy, roughhouse reputation for tough work and tougher lifestyles—days of hard fishing or cutting trees and nights full of women, dancing, and drinking—that had made Astoria what it was. On the other side were newer arrivals who saw the city as a decrepit place full of opportunity, so long as it could control its basest desires, curb the creeping influence of the Catholic Church and other minorities, and organize itself around the "100 percent Americanism" slogan.

There were debates and town hall meetings and an endless stream of newspaper editorials and letters to the editor. Households split and men fought. Churches closed ranks. The chamber of commerce nearly dissolved. Advertisements demonized anyone and everyone. Rumors of the worst kind were whispered and repeated.

Adding to the furor was a ballot measure in Oregon called the "Compulsory Education Act," requiring all students to attend public schools only. The real effect, so far as the Klan was concerned, would be the immediate shuttering of Catholic schools around the state.

"Rome will have to find a different job for the nuns that have been infecting our children for years on end in these parochial dens of indoctrination," Becker said in one of his *Western American* editorials. "We care not what job they do, so long as miles—possibly oceans—are placed between these papist 'servants' and the youngest minds of our grand state." The measure was hotly discussed around the state and in the streets and parlors of Astoria. There were even rumors that the governor, a secret supporter of the Klan, would be publicly supporting the measure.

The controversy finally boiled over one night when every window was smashed at St. Mary, Star of the Sea, the Catholic school perched on the hill of Fourteenth Street surrounded by ornate Victorian homes. The school's master, Father Sullivan, lashed out at the vandals in a letter to *The Morning Astorian*, calling them "Kowards in service of the Klan," and soon found himself with two broken ribs after being pulled into a stairwell on his way to mass the following Sunday. The incident made the newswires around the country, replete with critical mentions of the Ku Klux Klan and roiling tensions over the school-reform measure.

The day after the news broke, Becker took the train to Portland and entered the Klan office to find Giffords bickering over filing procedures with Darcy, who still did clerical work for him and occasionally answered the Klan's phones in the back of the store.

"Accounting duplicates belong with other accounting duplicates," Giffords was explaining in a petty voice. "And then we must be sure that the receipts are alphabetized in order—"

"I can't believe I'm here at the birthing place of such an impressive empire," she cut in. "Not only are you saving us from the grime of humanity—and I suppose I should include myself in that—but you're simultaneously standing up to the tyranny of disorganization. Fascinating."

"Don't get smart," Giffords shot back.

Becker, who had gone unnoticed in the doorway, finally spoke up, "Well I, for one, will stand with anyone putting their shoulder against the wheel to fight tyranny, clerical or otherwise."

Giffords was not amused, but he let it go and invited Becker into the office without pleasantries.

"What do you know about this episode with the Catholic school and this man Sullivan? Atlanta has been hassling me constantly," Giffords said, waving a newspaper in front of his face.

Becker tried to read Giffords's expression, searching for approval or disapproval but found neither. Becker cracked a half-smile. "I know that our good work is getting noticed. And notice feeds the hunger of recruitment. I've had five more men stop by the office in the past twenty-four hours, ready to join the effort."

Giffords seemed satisfied with that. Just then the phone rang, and he became lost in a new conversation. Becker followed Darcy out of the office and into another supply room at the back of the building crowded with giant bags of onions and other foodstuffs.

"Insufferable, isn't he?"

Darcy didn't respond, so Becker busied himself watching her shoulders and back tighten and release beneath her blouse as she adjusted boxes and cans on the shelves.

Finally she sighed and turned around with a box in both arms. "I think it's safe to say the whole thing is insufferable, but I don't suppose that's something you would agree with."

Becker put on his most pleasant face. "Let me take you to dinner and provide a thorough explanation. Or is that too insufferable of a prospect?"

"Actually, it is," she said, resuming her work. "I will say to you, Mr. Becker, that this line of work has allowed me to be privy to a good number of conversations between your grand dragon or whatever he's called and any number of people who phone or stop by to kiss his ring. Not only is he a toad, but he's an ass as well. Trust me on that score."

"I'll do you one better, Miss Darcy. The man dresses as though he's never seen a mirror."

She let out a short laugh but then caught herself.

"That should be the least of your concerns, Mr. Becker. Do you really endorse such an ugly purpose? I read the papers and I've heard the stories and I know exactly what's been done as part of your Invisible Empire. Broken bones. Men hanged. Families driven out of town without money or a place to stay, families that look just like mine. I suppose you're fine with that? You must be, since that's what fills the hours of your day and pays for your upkeep. But really, such a grotesque enterprise as the Ku Klux Klan?"

"The defense of American values is grotesque?"

She snorted. "If these are the values, then without doubt, yes."

His back stiffened. "I shine my light into whatever dark corner needs illuminating."

"Your light is a flame, Mr. Becker. You may tell yourself whatever story you wish—perhaps that you're a hero and a scholar and a noble soldier in some righteous cause." She took one step closer to him, her head trembling with anger. "But it's quite clear that you're lashing out against something that you can't actually see. You're not even sure what it is. Mr. Giffords as well. Both of you seem to think the world has turned on you, but it hasn't. At least not yet—men like you still rule. It pains me to say that, but I think men like you and Mr. Giffords are the ruin of things that are good."

Becker let out a long sigh and tried to smile. "You're not making a lick of sense, Miss Darcy."

She ignored him. "But there's one thing I suspect you already know: Your grip is starting to fail, and you know that when it does, you'll be left behind. And maybe that's what you fear the most, that you'll be abandoned with no one else to look after you, except the other damned fools in those ridiculous white robes of yours. That's going to be an awful lonely existence, I'm afraid. And somewhere inside that cavernous hole in your body, you know that." She shrugged and let it sink in. "Whatever it is that's eating at you in this world has left you wandering around like a stray dog, Mr. Becker, and you've joined the first vicious pack that would have you, just so you can have some sense of safety. Do you suppose that's true?"

A hurt look spread across his face for a tiny moment and then it was shed. "This is a tough game, and it's not for everyone. Today it's the Klan, and tomorrow perhaps it's someone else's turn, Miss Darcy, but the great machinery of America requires maintenance."

It was Becker who turned first for the door, but not before Darcy fired her parting shot. "The day I agree to let you take me to dinner is the day that I drop dead."

Back in Astoria the following week, Giffords barged into Becker's office like a compact ball of spinning energy and desire, tearing apart the calm of a wet morning. He came through the door mid-thought, it seemed.

"We know at this exact moment that what we have been trying to build now has a foundation. What's left to do is the framing—the walls, the floors, and the roof that will keep this structure sturdy and prepared for all nature of storms," he said, his eyes flashing. "We don't rest at moments like this, Mr. Becker. We move faster and stronger."

Becker was tired, though, and he was still a little stung by his conversation with Darcy. Now he was fighting bouts of indifference with *The Western American*. On a quiet afternoon the day before, he'd studied the ships anchored just outside his office window and wondered whether he should disappear at sea for a few years. Perhaps he could be captured as so many had been over the decades, shanghaied they'd called it, incapacitated by drink, then hustled onto a working ship only to wake up in the great vastness of the ocean, trapped in a life of forced maritime labor for years before finding a way home. It is sometimes easier, voluntarily or not, to turn your destiny over to others. *The dreams of an unambitious man*, Becker finally told himself, snapping to as the grand dragon held forth in his office. *Men like us are better than that.*

Giffords, apparently no longer troubled by the assault on the Catholic priest at Star of the Sea, had arrived with more money and read aloud a typed letter from headquarters in Atlanta: "Rather than shrink from controversy and recriminations, double down on Oregon's Klan. Push it harder, legitimize its purpose, marginalize its critics, and transform rebukes into opportunities for recruitment." It was happening in places like Indiana, Montana, and Idaho. Why not Oregon? There were personal rewards, too, Giffords told Becker: For Giffords, it was a chance to be the exalted cyclops of the entire western realm, and Becker could become the national leader for publicity with an office in Atlanta a few doors down from the imperial wizard.

"Remuneration in both of these positions is substantial and life-altering, as is the opportunity for preparing the country for real victory," Giffords read from the letter, which was unsigned but embossed with the Klan's elaborate seal.

Giffords salivated at his chance for rewards, reciting the letter out loud twice and pausing for dramatic effect at several places. He then made a show of closing the door in Becker's office and moving the two of them to the center of the room. A sea lion belched from the river below, but the air was silent otherwise. Giffords laid his idea out in whispers, something momentous and transformative for Astoria and the empire—a fire, a city cast into crisis, citizens desperate for hope and leadership, then an opportunity for Klan members, newly elected to city government, to rebuild Astoria greater than it ever was. Every new city block would be a fortress in testament to the Klan's management and civic legitimacy. When Giffords was done he smiled wide and stepped back with his arms spread wide, giddy for Becker's reaction.

"It certainly is bold," Becker said, trying to summon some enthusiasm. "And foolish."

"The Visigoths certainly never let that stop them when they were on Rome's doorstep, did they?"

Becker twisted his face in slight confusion at the analogy but took the point. "Certainly not."

"Good man. I'll leave it to you to put this in motion," Giffords said, gathering his coat and putting his hand on Becker's shoulder. "Your father would be proud."

The grand dragon was out the door before Becker, stunned, had a chance to stop him.

In early November 1922 the Klan's slate of candidates won easily on election night. Just like the special election to oust Sheriff Nelson that summer, Becker and others spent weeks twisting arms, threatening blackmail, passing envelopes of cash into coat pockets, and warning some to simply stay home on Election Day. "Home is always the safest place," Becker had become fond of saying. The new mayor and council members would take office in January. *The Astorian-Budget* and *The Morning Astorian* were apoplectic, fearing the end of the great city at the mouth of the Columbia.

"Becker and his ilk have so divided this city that we may never return to who we once were," *The Morning Astorian* editorialized. "These are no mere battle scars from an election hard-fought but rather a disease let loose among us whose only cure may be time, and that is if we are lucky."

Becker responded with a letter to both papers, heaping high-handed praise on the losing candidates for a race well-run. "Now is the time to come together. The most difficult times are those ahead, and I have the fullest confidence that the city's new governing fathers will impress, inspire, and—yes, friends—heal this mighty but fractured city."

Late on the Friday night after the elections, Becker locked his office door and had taken two steps on the sidewalk when a searing light doused his face, obscuring everything else in view. There was a scuffle as he was shoved against the building and a lamp hovered just a few inches from his nose.

"For Christ's sake, will you turn that off?" Becker said, blinking against the blinding yellow light. "There's no need to—"

A wooden sap came down hard on his forehead. He could feel wetness at the wound, immediately cooled by the breeze.

"You're not talking," came a low voice. It was thick and foreign around the edges. Becker could see the forms of two, possibly three, tall men somewhere behind the light. "This deserves your full attention, and that can't happen if your mouth is moving. What you've done . . ."

The man behind the voice shifted his weight against Becker, stalling for time to gather thoughts that perhaps should've been gathered before this meeting.

"These little antics that have been performed by you and those in your Ku Klux Klan have become disruptive. Now . . . there are sometimes benefits that come with disruption, one must only look to—"

"This isn't a lecture," another gruff voice interrupted. "You either make this right or begin contemplating a life without the tips of your fingers. Is that understood?"

The men closed in tighter around Becker, all bulky coats and meaty breaths.

"Am I talking now?" Becker smiled, his eyes now closed against the light and the ache in his head. "Because if I am, I will say that, admittedly, I'm a bit unclear on what remedy is being sought here."

Just then a group of noisy drunks spilled out of a door just down the block. The confrontation paused, and Becker began considering who was accosting him. *A sore loser from the election? Some hapless bootlegger who'd lost skin in the sheriff's crackdown? An errant member of the Invisible Empire? Had the Knights of Columbus finally found their manhood and decided to get their hands dirty?* Somewhere inside there was a flash of perverse pleasure that the list could be so long.

"The remedy," Becker hissed after the distraction. "What the hell do you want?"

Another pulse of people spilled onto the street. Becker heard one of the men begin to speak and then think twice. Instead the answer came with a sudden punch to the gut that left him on his knees and doubled over on the sidewalk, listening as footsteps walked off into the darkness. He felt the cloud-clogged night sky above him slowly spin clockwise and then in reverse. Somehow the motion unlocked a thought about his father, perhaps Giffords's offhand mention had triggered it. *How had he even known?* Becker had a vision of his father standing high on a hill in front of a large crowd with his fists above his head and a burning cross off to one side. His voice was hoarse from yelling, but the men in front of him were rapt. "Every tree relies on its branches, even the smallest ones, to remain strong and growing," his father said. "Even you."

Not far off, a sea lion barked in the night, shaking Becker out of his reverie.

Chapter 21

1922

A few days after he was attacked, Lem Becker found John G. Smith through the Loyal Legion of Loggers and Lumbermen. It was a farce of an organization, a "labor" group formed by the wealthiest timber barons in an attempt to counteract the unrest fomented by the Wobblies and others calling for better wages and better conditions. Smith had signed up for the legion during a mandatory gathering between the lumberjacks at Olney camp and a group of surly men who'd come to Olney from Seattle on behalf of the lumber company. They went from man to man, ordering them to fill out the form as part of their duties as employees and residents of America. Smith thought little of it, assuming it was yet another condition for staying employed.

Becker was given the roster by a kleagle who had underlined several names of men who might be good prospects for the Invisible Empire, men with names that sounded American and protestant. Becker kept the purpose of the list to himself after talking with the kleagle and thanked him with a small bit of cash, promising more if he could provide additional information on a few of the men. As a result Becker learned that Smith was Scandinavian, had a sister in trouble with the city police, and sometimes associated with men at the *Toveri* and several other radical organizations. Becker arranged a special trip out to the woods of Olney and the timber camp.

"I'm not sure that I see a future Klansman sitting in front of me," Becker said to Smith when they finally met on the arrangement of the logging camp's manager, a new Klansman himself, eager to make an impression. "That's a special cut of man who comes along only every once in a while. You don't fit the bill, but don't feel bad about that."

Smith's eyes wandered over Becker's suit and silk tie and eventually settled on the unexplained purple welt on his forehead. Becker shooed the camp manager away from their meeting spot, a clearing in the trees not far from the bunkhouse, and indicated that he needed a private conversation with the skinny timberman, Smith.

"I do have occasion for some help outside the organization though," Becker continued once they were alone. "Tasks that need the right sort of person with the appropriate level of discretion and derring-do."

"I have plenty to do up here," Smith said softly. "Still many, many trees yet to cut."

"Good wages, then?"

Smith shrugged. "Plenty enough. We've got a place to sleep and food to eat and something left over at the end of the week, so I fare just fine."

Now it was Becker who paused to look over Smith, with his brown straight hair coming to his eyebrows and expressionless face—the sort of man who passes through a crowd without notice except by those who might be looking for him.

"And Lily? Do you have the means to extract her from the fix she's in?"

Smith's back stiffened. "What do you know of my sister?"

"Plenty."

Becker offered vague outlines of his proposal to Smith, searching his eyes for any sign of agreement or distress but found them empty and inscrutable, like knots in a board. When they parted, Becker gave him a hard pat on the shoulder and a sour smile that those in Smith's home country would have been wary of. *Warm waters on top hide cold currents beneath*, they would say back home. Becker vowed to call on Smith when he was needed, with no indication of when that would be and only a promise that he would make it worth his while.

Becker returned to Olney a couple of weeks later. The logging camp was slicked with mud, and he was careful to step over the most treacherous spots in his leather Oxfords. A foreman pointed toward a shed near the back of the camp where Smith, dirty and sweating, was repairing a choker chain.

"Still engaged in the high art of tree cutting," Becker said. "It's good to know your calling, of course."

Smith hadn't seen Becker since his last visit but wasn't surprised upon his return. He'd been waiting and, in a small way, hoping. Lily had been in jail for months over the killing of the *Iowan* crewman and had a trial coming up that would almost certainly send her to the state prison in Salem.

In a stand of trees beyond the shed, Becker detailed the plan and then repeated it one more time, almost verbatim, placing special emphasis on some of the key details. There was no explanation about why his task was called for—certainly its magnitude caught him a little off-guard—and Becker was careful to avoid any opening in their conversation that might lead to that.

"So as you see, there are some logistical elements to this but nothing very onerous," Becker said. "Any questions on how to carry this out?"

Smith felt the weight of his own body sink inescapably deeper into the ground, like an animal caught in a ditch full of hot tar. He thought about Lily waiting for some miracle in her cell as the days of her life ticked away. He thought about the crime he was being asked to commit. "I understand it fine and can do it without trouble. But first I must know what the exact value is for me."

"Splendid. The value for you, my friend, is threefold. Cash payment of $1,000 delivered once the assignment is complete. I can also arrange for you to finally leave this camp and take a job with the city—nothing glamorous, to be sure, but certainly far better and easier and more lucrative than you'll get here. And finally, your sister is led out of trouble. The case against her can easily fall apart so she can be sprung from her cage and start anew. What she does after that is not my concern, but at least she will be out of the fix she's in now and you can steward her toward something better, I would hope."

"She's going on trial. She's supposed to be in court—"

"I'm fully aware of where she is in the procedural process, Mr. Smith. I'm saying I can take care of that."

Smith nodded quietly. "How do I know that if I do this task for you, you'll keep your word?"

"You don't, and I don't know that you'll keep your word either, do I? But sometimes the universe requires faith to get what we want, wouldn't you say?" Becker pulled a small roll of money out of his pocket and opened Smith's hand to place it in his palm. "Faith also requires evidence along the way, Mr. Smith. Let's call this a start toward getting what we both want."

Smith didn't bother to count the money but instinctively sensed it was a large amount and pushed it deep into his pants pocket.

"It goes without saying, but I'll say it anyway: There are grave consequences for discussing this ever again," Becker said, his face growing serious. "There are a good many ways this degenerates into undesired outcomes for you and your sister. I could certainly allow her case to proceed and certainly have you taken off this job and bring your name—and associations with our friends at the *Toveri*—to the correct authorities who would be grateful for such intelligence."

Becker let his threats sink in.

"But that's not my preference and certainly isn't your preference, I know."

Smith shrugged. "I have nothing to do with the *Toveri*."

"I know that you owed them money and that you have paid them money. We have their ledgers. It's an ugly thing to be caught up in their politics, Mr. Smith. Not terribly American, if you ask me."

"That was a long time ago, and it was a personal matter. Politics had nothing to do with it."

"Not long enough. And politics always matter, I'm afraid," Becker said with a half-smile. "I've found that every decision we make in life, Mr. Smith, is a political one. At its root, I mean. Which store we shop at. Which moving picture we see. Who we talk to when we go downtown. Even which gal we ask to dance. They all connect to a deeper part of us that is guided by our beliefs. And each of those decisions over a lifetime strings together a *system* of beliefs. And all belief systems become political. It can't be helped."

A cold fog was settling into the trees around them, and in the distance the men at the camp were cackling around the fire at a joke that Smith couldn't hear. The two men parted on uneasy terms, and Smith found his way to the fire but was in no mood to laugh.

Becker came back to the camp in Olney two nights later with a grim face. He drove Smith to a pullout near the Youngs River in a clearing surrounded by Doug firs and a fresh carpet of ferns. Becker laid out the plan again, this time including the date and the exact location. The job would only take a few minutes, but the benefits would last far beyond, he reminded Smith. There was the remainder of the cash that would be paid afterward plus the possibility of a job with the city, and Lily's criminal case would come to a quiet but favorable end.

"She's out of trouble forever?" Smith asked.

"For as long as she keeps her nose clean or leaves town. All I can guarantee is that this case in Clatsop County finds a way to die. I can't provide eternal forgiveness beyond that."

Smith had visited Lily the day before at the downtown jail. He couldn't bear to ask who'd given her a black eye or about the new crick in her neck. It was clear enough, though, that she was not capable of taking care of herself in Astoria, inside the jail, or outside on the streets. He didn't mention his visits with this man from the city.

"Then I need passage for her back to Finland," Smith continued to Becker. "If she stays here, the hardships will continue, and she will either die or rot away in jail, and that is as good as killing her."

"There's money enough for that in your payment," Becker said.

"The money is only part of it. It's the papers and the arrangements. You know what it's like to make a trip like that. She needs documents to travel, documents to secure her as a citizen back in her home country."

"That's beyond what I can do and was never part of our discussion," Becker disputed, feeling his blood start to pump.

"She cannot stay," Smith said and set his jaw. "She has to go home."

"The terms are the terms."

The two stood facing each other, and the afternoon rain eased. The cold dampness hung around them with nowhere else to go.

"Then I cannot help," Smith said, waving one hand.

Becker grabbed him by the shoulders and pushed him back against the car, but Smith had the animal strength of years of work in the woods. He quickly spun Becker around and drove him into the wet ground, bearing down on his chest and pinning his arms. Becker cussed and squirmed but couldn't get out. Finally, with Smith's hands now tightly gripping the collars of the man's coat, he relaxed his body and tried to draw in a full breath.

"You have two real options here, Mr. Smith," Becker said, laboring to get the words out. "You either complete this job as agreed—and accept the more-than-generous terms we've already discussed—or you . . ."

Growing angrier, Smith let his weight settle further into Becker's chest.

"—Or you and your sister find yourselves on the wrong side of every kind of trouble you can imagine." He paused to get a breath. "We've got people that can link you to the Reds or ship you off to a prison somewhere for sedition or make sure your sister's next jail meal has enough strychnine to down a horse." Becker winced again. "Trust me when I say these options are all within our grasp should we need them." He felt Smith's hot breath on his face and tried to smile. "I'd like nothing more than to make this work for both of us, but there are limits. Don't let the lack of a perfect bargain get in the way of one that still has significant merit, Mr. Smith."

Smith finally relented, and they drove back to Olney in silence, but he refused to shake Becker's hand before getting out of the car.

"We have a deal?"

"It will be done," he said. "But please, I beg you, find a way to send Lily home."

Part 5 *Combustion*

Chapter 22

1922

Of all people, it was the fire chief's wife who warned him the city would burn.

"You don't build a city on kindling and not expect a fire to destroy the whole damn thing in one fell swoop," she had told her husband, Charles E. Foster, one night, years before the winter of 1922. "You're a fool if you do."

Chief Foster was a young firefighter the first time Astoria burned in 1883, when sparks at the Clatsop Mill leaped into a pile of planer shavings. He and his crew were there within minutes, but it was already hopeless: Flames skipped from building to building and snaked beneath the streets. They had only a single fire truck and a hose that sucked water from the river and laid it on the flames in an anemic trickle.

"C'mon, I piss more than this!" one of his crewmates had shouted.

Within a few hours, the sawmill, two docks, and every business on Commercial Street between Fourteenth and Seventeenth had been razed. The next day Foster was assigned to the local vigilance committee to keep looters away. One thief caught with an armful of tools from the mill's partially burned shed was hustled to the cemetery and told that he could choose between being hanged or whipped. When the man refused to decide, Foster was told to wrap a rope around the man's neck and loop it over the tree. Foster got a single loop over his head before the man settled on a whipping.

The city, impatient and ambitious, rushed to rebuild. The remaining sawmills worked double-time to cut planks, and crews were brought in from Portland to restore Astoria to what it had been: tightly crammed with wood-framed buildings that were perched atop timber pilings over the squishy shore of the Columbia River. Connecting them all was a network of wooden streets. The building technique left a series of open channels beneath the streets and buildings, perfect for delivering fire from one end of town to the other and every block between. Foster's wife had warned him, and he'd warned the city fathers, but no one seemed interested in the least.

"If you have time to spare, Chief Foster, to secure us an ample supply of sand or other material to lay beneath our city, then by all means, please proceed," the mayor had told him. "Meanwhile we are getting on with the business of rebuilding our city far better than before. And quickly."

City leaders had long nursed the dream of being a premier port along the West Coast, ready to rival Seattle and San Francisco. "Venice of the West," some liked to say. Construction methods would have to be fought over some other time. The one improvement the city had made incrementally over the years as Foster rose through the ranks and became fire chief was a series of fire hydrants posted on several street corners that tapped into the city's water mains. It was something.

Charles Foster retired as the fire chief in 1921, but by December 1922, the city had yet to find his replacement. So he still slept next to an alarm and a phone.

The night of the fire had been quiet for a Friday. The chill had kept most people home—that and the fact that the Hammond Mill had burned that fall and left nine hundred men without a paycheck to spend at the end of the week. The drizzle seemed to be putting a cap on the night.

The Blue Mouse Theatre, newly opened a few months earlier, was only half-full for its showing of *What's Wrong with Women?* Up the street, the Dreamland had a dance. The band got drunk and there were a few scuffles but nothing unusual. After midnight the nine cops on duty made their final rounds through Uppertown, Uniontown, downtown, Chinatown, the canneries, and up through the hills where most of the town slept and rain fell soundlessly. A few drunks were cleared off the sidewalks, some prostitutes too. The copious Christmas lights strung high above the street from one block to another were unplugged.

The first call came in at 2:12 a.m.: flames spotted beneath Thiel's Pool Hall on Commercial Street where a few stragglers had stuck around to play and sneak a few last sips. At the same time a few doors down, fire had erupted in the Palace Café. Between the pool hall and the café was the Bee Hive department store, the perennial hub of retail, with its front windows decked out for Christmas and full of toys.

The alarm rang at all four fire stations and the home of every volunteer. The five short rings, which hadn't been heard since the Hammond mill burned, added an extra shot of adrenaline.

From the closest station, crews hopped into the new Stutz fire engine, picked up Foster at his home, and sped to the heart of downtown. Hooking up to a hydrant at Twelfth and Commercial, the crew ran their hose to Thiel's, where flames were tearing around the basement—a place for storing wood and coal—and growing with each second. At Foster's order, the men tossed back the wooden trap door to the basement and were met with a sickening blast of heat that knocked the helmets off their heads and forced them into retreat.

By then the fire was ripping through the adjoining basement of the Bee Hive. The crew from the station at Fourth and Astor arrived, and Foster sent two men with their hose beneath the building. The flames had already reached the floor above them and part of it collapsed, raining a heap of goods onto both men, who quickly climbed up the hose back to the surface.

"What the hell was that?" one of them said when they reached the street.

"God telling us to smarten up and get out of there," the other replied, trembling.

The view from the street was horrifying. By 2:30 a.m. the pool hall and the café had been eaten by flames and the buildings across the street, still wet from the rain, were already steaming from the radiating heat. Up and down the block, windows shattered and walls groaned as if they were being eaten alive. The roar of the flames filled the night air. The firemen tried to lay in with their hoses, only to see their supply suddenly cut short when the twelve-inch water main, perched on wooden blocks at Eleventh and Commercial, melted and then burst.

Foster felt his heart sink and stepped away from his men for a moment, half-tempted to keep walking, pull out his crews, and let everything burn. Might serve the city's fathers right and keep a few of his men from getting killed for, what, this scuffling little empire fraught with booze and drugs and petty politics? Maybe a fresh start would do some good. Hot fires have a way of burning out lingering imperfections. But this had been his home for most of his life, for better and for worse.

Within minutes all twenty-two men—including twelve full-time regulars and ten "extras"—were with Foster on the street, along with every piece of equipment he had: the Stutz pumper, three American La France combination trucks, a Dodge fire truck, and several thousand feet of hose. Foster knew that if the flames began traveling through the interlocking galleries beneath the city streets, they'd be sunk. Fire was predictable in many ways—it relied on the simple combination of combustion: fuel and oxygen—but a gust of wind or sudden change in conditions could force the fire through the city's underground tunnels, unseen till it exploded at the surface.

Foster and his men spent a few more minutes attacking the fire on Commercial, trying desperately to save the Bee Hive, Owl Drug, the Liberty Theatre, and the Merwyn Hotel, but were quickly pushed off the block and north, toward the river, to Bond Street.

By then most of the town was awake, and a crowd gathered downtown, some dressed, some still in their sleeping clothes. Initially most came to gawk, figuring the fire would be out soon enough. There had been dozens of fires in Astoria that year, but most had been efficiently cut short by Foster's men.

Tonight's fire was a beast, though, and it was going to have its say. Dampened by hoses in one place, flames popped up in another, blooming wildly from beneath streets and finding new life with every unburned slab of timber in its path. Brick buildings scattered downtown should've checked the flames, but they were soon lit up too. So were the wooden streets whose asphalt coating only melted and produced a putrid smoke before collapsing altogether.

One block fell and then another and another after that. The fighting became more frantic and feverish, driven by a roiling sense of hopelessness. Foster felt his chest tighten as he ran through several blocks to another crew, living every fireman's nightmare. Someone in the crowd called for dynamite. Blow up a few buildings in the fire's path, the thinking went, and you rob it of fuel to continue its march. The prospect excited the crowd, nervous and desperate for anything that might get the flames under control. Foster objected, "I'm a fire chief, not a dynamiter."

They ignored him. Someone in the city retrieved a batch of dynamite and began setting it off in buildings around the fire. They were weak explosives, though, shattering only the windows and providing yet another way for the fire to enter and continue its work. Someone else drove out of town toward one of the logging camps where more powerful dynamite was used to blow out stumps. Soon enough, deafening concussions shattered the night air every few minutes, demolishing walls and streets and anything else in the way.

Electricity failed, gas lines burst and caught flame, and inevitably the hoses didn't reach, or when they did they were limp and without water. Foster wondered if the water supply been cut off. Pumps siphoned water from the river and shot it through hoses, but it was never enough. A Stutz caught fire and exploded.

By 3:30 a.m. the fire had reached "Automobile Row" on Duane Street and was closing in on the Weinhard Hotel and Astoria National Bank. Foster was there when Norris Staples tried to push one of his cars out of harm's way and dropped dead of a failed heart in the lot. They'd been schoolmates at one point, and now Staples had slumped to the street, deaf to any calls to get out. As he knelt beside Staples, Foster looked up to see the silhouette of two men in the smoke-filled law offices above the bank building. They'd opened up the windows and were tossing books, ledgers, and boxes of papers out onto the streets—many of which were caught up in the swirling waves of heat and ash and were then swiftly consumed.

The fire was moving at will on the west end, where there was no water at all to fight it. Foster heard more dynamite blasts and shook his head, sure that the city was on its last legs. Small victories arrived, though. A river dredger pulled up on the waterfront and doused an entire city block, staving off the flames and keeping disaster from rushing into many of the canneries and oil tanks that supplied local ships. An army of nurses and neighbors evacuated patients from St. Mary's Hospital and took them farther up the hill to the high school. A group of boys carried medicine and equipment there too, and fire crews from Portland spent the rest of the night making sure the hospital survived. Not far off, three men with a single hose spent more than an hour spraying water on the telephone exchange, saving a critical line of communication to the rest of the world. The men then turned the hose to *The Astorian-Budget* next door. It stood for fifteen more minutes before finally bursting into flame.

Icy rain turned to snow and back to rain again as the night wore on. As the sense of catastrophe set in, panicked store owners rifled through their businesses, pulling out the most expensive items and loading them first on street corners and later into trucks to be taken to the edge of downtown. Some piles of rugs and furniture and clothes weren't moved fast enough and burned where they'd been left.

Apartment buildings disappeared into a heap of ash, as did the Weinhard Hotel and several boarding houses. Astoria National Bank eventually burned too, leaving the face of its giant clocked blistered at 4:20 a.m. The wind shifted to the east and pushed the fire toward the riverside, with its warehouses and docks still piled high with crates. The tugboat *Oneonta* pulled up to the docks. A young crewman from Norway, Carl Jacob Korneliuson, attempted to jump ashore but, in the noise and confusion, misjudged the distance. He fell into the black river and drowned.

Nearby, men with dynamite arrived at the Lovell Auto Company, ready to blast it away to stop the fire's creep. The owner ran them off the property with a rifle in his hands, and somehow his building survived.

Foster went from block to block, herding people out of the way, trying to discern between shouts of terror and real pain. Finally the noise in his ears settled into a low roar and the hours became a blur. He helped where he could, training hoses, repairing equipment, and barking commands to his crews. Inside, though, he felt himself slipping into the darkness, like being submerged in a bathtub that never stopped filling.

The windows of the ornate and colorful Victorian houses on the hill overlooking downtown Astoria were full of backlit spectators, with their arms folded and backs hunched against the horrors unfolding below.

It was well after 7 a.m. when the first edges of gray sunlight appeared on the eastern horizon. Foster walked through town alone. Nearly every block that had been built on stilts, some thirty-two in all, was either burning or smoldering in utter defeat and ruin. He'd never been a religious man, so he simply fell to his knees, in the middle of a city he no longer recognized, and wept.

Chapter 23

1922

Looters found their way to downtown Astoria as soon as news broke about the big fire. The first thirty-six hours were a free-for-all as men, women, and children picked their way through the rubble, stuffing jewelry, clothes, books, papers—anything they could find that seemed remotely valuable—into their coats and bags. Some brought bedsheets downtown, spread them out on the ground, covered them with pilfered goods, wrapped them up, and carried them away on their shoulders.

The police were outnumbered. Stick-wielding store owners spent hours guarding the remains of their businesses, but the thieves took advantage of the cold, the lack of electricity, and the long nights due to the winter darkness. The National Guard finally arrived at the end of the second day, assigning two armed men to every safe they could find. Most had survived the fire, but the heat had seared the metal so badly that none could be opened. It would be days before the first experts arrived to take them apart.

Small new fires occasionally cropped up as oxygen found its way to some bit of smoldering wood and produced a hiss and a flame and usually prompted someone to run over with a shovel or bucket of water.

H. H. Flemming returned to Astoria the week between Christmas and New Year's. Someone had laced a few feeble strings of lights over Commercial Street, stretching from the pile of rubble where the Liberty Theatre once stood to the hole in the ground that used to be Hansen's Shoes. It was still afternoon, but the winter light was already fading, and the white holiday lights sparkled like a handful of diamonds floating in the winter air.

"Gestures still mean something," came a voice behind Flemming as she ducked beneath the Christmas lights and into a wet pile of ash to examine what was left of the fire hydrant on the corner. The voice was from the outgoing mayor, a ruddy-faced man named Bremmer. "In fact they mean more in the darkest times."

Flemming turned to face the mayor and smiled. "Just the man I was hoping to see."

The mayor had been insisting in the papers that the blaze had been started by "a firebug firmly in the ranks of the Reds, radicals who think they can begin a revolution where I live." A day later, a story in the paper detailed how someone had broken into the city's public works director's house the night of the fire and cut his phone lines, and that the water lines feeding downtown had been sabotaged somewhere along the way.

"These rats have gone too far this time," the mayor was quoted in the story. "They've overplayed their hand and now it's time to make them pay."

Flemming fished a notebook and pen from her coat pocket. "Sounds like your men have been doing some bang-up work investigating our fire. Suspects abound, I gather. I'd love to get some names so I can complete my work here. Would you indulge me?"

The mayor wrinkled his nose and shook his head. "We've got it handled thus far. Not that we don't appreciate your efforts."

"I'm an officer of the state," Flemming said, realizing that her head had been pounding ever since she'd arrived earlier in the day. Too much bourbon went down easy the night before. "The city and its officers, including the office of the mayor, have an obligation to aid and cooperate in this investigation. The law is quite clear that—"

"Of course, of course," the mayor said, patting Flemming on the shoulder. "In due time, ma'am, you'll have our fullest cooperation. Allow us to find our way and you'll get everything you need."

"I'm under no obligation to wait. The full force of—"

The mayor was already turning to walk away. "Justice will be done, Inspector Flemming. Fear not."

The next day Flemming followed the information that the Chinese man in the sauna had given her. She didn't know the dentist's name, but she wasn't hard to find. Asta Blomquist was at her temporary office in a stone building coated in soot and ash on the corner of Eighth and Astor, next door to the temporary offices of *The Morning Astorian*. She was hesitant and distracted at first, pretending to sort through a blackened stack of files that a local businessman had found and delivered to her in a box. Flemming introduced herself and waited for the woman to focus.

"Everything I had at my practice is gone," the dentist said finally. She picked up the files and two small metal tools that looked like wires and held them delicately like they were dead birds. "This is what I have left," Asta muttered, holding them up for her to see. "I'm starting over with *this*."

Flemming mumbled an apology and hoped the dentist couldn't smell the beer on her breath from lunch at Liz's. She didn't look like a dentist, Flemming decided, at least not the kind of twisted soul who would inflict agony on you and insist that it was for your own good. She was pretty, brunette, and sure of herself in a way that seemed unconcerned about the opinions of most. Flemming liked her straightaway.

Asta moved her head back a little to take in the tall woman standing in front of her.

"You investigate fires?"

"You pull teeth?" Flemming shot back.

"I suppose I do," Asta said.

"Same here. I've got stories, but I'm sure you've got a few dingers yourself."

Asta smiled and shook her head in dismay. "You wouldn't believe what some of these men do when they get in my chair. Disgusting. And some days I don't bother to numb the pain as much as I could, if you know what I mean."

Flemming tilted her head back and let out a delighted laugh. "Such immediate repercussions. I love it. We should all be so lucky."

"It's a living." Asta shrugged.

"So I hear you had a visitor the night of the fire," Flemming said. "Care to spill on that?"

The dentist waited a couple of beats and let out a sigh. "I'd rather not, actually."

"No?"

Asta twisted the band on her finger. "Are you married?"

Flemming chuckled halfheartedly. "Who'd turn down a chance for this glamorous showstopper? Tall, mouthy, working all the time, and maybe a little too loose with my recreational abuses. Did I mention that I often smell of soot and can't seem to stay clean for very long?"

Asta nodded. "Well, regardless, I'm sure you have a fairly decent working knowledge of marital complications," she said. "Perhaps even a little forgiveness for them?"

Flemming pulled a notebook from her wool overcoat. "The night of the fire?"

"It was late," Asta began. "I was in the apartment that my husband and I share—shared, just a couple blocks from my office. We have a house just over there on Irving." She pointed up the hill behind her. "I'd taken the apartment when I first moved to town but kept it after we got married. I sometimes slept there after a late night, and my husband often did the same. I guess it's gone now too. Anyway, the night of the fire, I was up reading, and someone barged in like he'd taken a run at the door—"

"This man, he was someone you—"

"I'll get to that. So he broke through the door and took a couple of steps inside with this look on his face like he was a wild animal but also like his eyes were vacant; it was the strangest thing. He looked at me dead-on and said, 'I've just lit the downtown on fire. You'll see soon enough.' And then he ran out again. Sure enough, not long after, everything was on fire."

"Did you know this man?"

Asta nodded. "It was Bart Layton. We grew up together in Knappton, across the river, but I hadn't seen him for years."

"Were you friends?"

"Not exactly," she said slowly, gathering herself. "He was sweet on me a long time ago, but it never went anywhere and then he stopped writing and then he just disappeared. It was nothing. Boy stuff."

"Are you sure it was him?"

"I'm sure of it. He looked different, as I say, he was wild, but it was the same fellow."

Asta explained the notes under her pillow in Knappton, the surprise visit in The Dalles, the subsequent letters from Tacoma, and the increasingly bizarre ones mailed from Montana with sentiments she had a hard time deciphering. Until his recent reappearance, she hadn't seen him for years.

Flemming felt a charge through her bloodstream that perhaps the net was finally tightening around a suspect. Good leads gave her the kind of energy bursts that cocaine gave the dopers, she often thought, and were perhaps just as addicting, albeit more elusive.

"So you and he never—"

"No. Never. And now that I'm married, well, that's fairly well out of the question, isn't it?"

The inspector leaned in. "So why would he show up suddenly and start a fire at the Bee Hive?"

"My office was above the store," she said and then dimmed her voice into a thin ribbon of exhaustion. "I have no idea what he was thinking."

Asta folded into a chair and the color washed out of her face as she surveyed the destruction around her. Flemming's mind raced, trying to piece together a motive and opportunity for arson. *Unrequited love suddenly rekindled, then rebuffed, then a revenge fire is set? Plausible. But hasn't it been years since this puppy love was aflame? Still, heartache has a way of hanging on, festering into darker intent if left untreated for too long.*

"Did your husband know this fellow? This history the two of you had?"

Asta nodded slowly, folding her hands in her lap. "Yes, what little there is of it."

"And of this man Layton's visit to you the night of the fire?"

"Of course. He was none too pleased."

"But neither of you reported this to the police?" Flemming tried to swallow her frustration. "You had the arsonist in your house, a man you knew, and kept it to yourselves?"

Asta sighed and folded her hands in her lap. "It's more complicated than that."

Flemming kept quiet to let her continue.

"Frederick's in the running for a seat on the state dentistry board. It's now between him and another dentist, from Klamath Falls, I think. Very close."

Flemming let out a laugh. "So, we're not trying to upset this very delicate apple cart? For a seat on the state board of dentists? That's a hell of an excuse—"

"How does it look to have a strange man coming into your home and confessing a crime to your wife in the middle of the night?" Asta challenged. "Especially when you're not home."

"And where was Frederick?"

Asta shook her head and her face hardened. "In a card room on Bond Street. Doing God knows what . . ."

"Doing what a man who wants to be on the state dentistry board probably ought not to be doing," Flemming finished.

Upon returning to Astoria the first week of January 1923, Flemming spent a week looking for Bart Layton. On the second day she found his mother and stepfather at their place on Seventeenth Street. It was a blue, one-bedroom house balanced on the hillside with a crooked view of the Columbia. They met Flemming at the door.

"He comes and goes like a dog with no sense of when to get out of the rain," Ole Estoos said, responding to Flemming's first question. "Mostly he goes, I'd say. And keeps his mother in a mighty agitated state, half-worried to death."

His mother nodded, inviting Flemming out of the doorway and into the house.

"He's not been right for some time," she said. "He takes care of himself, mostly by thieving and getting himself tossed into jail when it suits him. But at least then I know he's eating. What's this about?"

Flemming motioned toward downtown Astoria, where the blackened wreck of buildings stood out against the gray layer hanging above them. "Any chance he could've been responsible for that?" she asked gingerly.

Bart's mom gasped, put her arm around her husband, then looked back at Flemming. "Not a chance," she said sternly. "He's a lot of things, there's no escaping that, but he's no fire starter. People *died* in that fire and that's just not his nature, ill-suited as he might be to civilized society."

"Okay, okay, sure."

"A mother knows her children," she continued. "And he'd never do that."

Flemming tried to explain, "Well, there are times when accidents turn into something that—"

"What brings this line of suspicion onto Bart?" Ole interrupted.

The investigator had learned it was best not to broadcast her leads and where they came from. People talk, word spreads, suspects disappear, stories change, too many things go south, and cases evaporate.

"Just routine to canvass the area, check out any known criminals, get them eliminated from suspicion. So that's what this is about today. Any idea of where I might find him?"

Worry remained on the mother's face. "Not a clue. Here? Across the river? Portland? For crying out loud, he was in Montana last year if you can believe that."

Flemming turned for the door, but Bart Layton's mom stopped her before she went outside.

"He didn't do this," she said, looking dead into Flemming's eyes. "And if you see him, tell him . . . that his mother loves him. Will you do that?"

Flemming spent the evening in a beer room and the night in a woman's boarding house not far from the river. A winter rain soaked everything and bore down on the roof, hard and then harder, like it had found an extra gear. As she slipped from the fog of drunkenness into the fog of sleep, she puzzled over the irony of how a city that was perpetually rained upon could be destroyed by fire. Her last conscious thought was that there was a fine poetry to it, a sonnet she had yet to unravel. She made a note to deliver that bit of literary wisdom to her sister when she got back to Portland but promptly forgot when sleep overtook her.

The next day Flemming took the small ferry across the Columbia to the Washington side of the river and paid for a ride to Knappton, the logging town and quarantine station dug into the river's edge with a vast forest at its back. At the town's lone café there were clusters of Chinese, Finns, Germans, and even a few Spaniards hunched over a long wooden table in the middle of the room that was cluttered with soup tureens, bread loaves, and water pitchers. The men slurped and chewed and talked and paid no attention to Flemming when she entered. Hardly any spoke English, and none of them claimed to know Bart Layton when she asked. It was the same with the waitresses, the mill manager, and the nurses at the quarantine station. Finally, at the post office, a building so small Flemming felt like she had to hold her breath to fit into it, the stooped man behind the counter rose straight and tall when Flemming mentioned Bart's name.

"He's a damned thief," the man said before hoisting a burlap sack of envelopes onto the counter to be sorted. He paused as if he might apologize for his salty tone in front of a woman but thought better of it when he saw she was as big as a man and had the look of someone who'd been in more than a few coarse situations.

Flemming let out a sigh of relief that perhaps the trip across the river hadn't been a complete bust.

The man stopped what he was doing, rubbed his bald head, and made a show of stroking both ends of his stringy red mustache before folding his arms across his chest. "And I'll tell you what's more. The little runt probably still has the spectacles he stole. From my father right down the road here. So I remember him, yes. And do you know what happened? This was quite some time ago, but this is what happened: My pappy lost his spectacles and stepped off the pier down there, just walked straight off and died, drowned in the goddamned river. Not long after his specs went missing. Because he couldn't see for shit."

"When was this?"

"Fifteen, twenty years back."

"And you're sure it was him?"

The retelling of the episode had left the man emotional and laboring with shallow breaths. "He damned well did it. There's no proving it, of course, but everyone here had something that disappeared and found its way into his greasy hands. I can guaran-damn-tee pappy's specs went the same way."

"Do you ever see Bart around?"

"Oh, I think he pretty well knows not to darken this side of the river too much. I've told most everyone that if I see him, I'll have his head and his ass too."

Flemming spent the rest of the day in Knappton. No one else had seen this elusive thief and alleged arsonist. On the boat back to Astoria, long after dark, Flemming stood in the bow and let the pungent sea mist pummel her hair and face. "He's a goddamn ghost," she said into the wet air.

Flemming spent most of the next day in a borrowed office at the police station. The desk sergeant had a scant file on Layton: his arrest from shoplifting at the Bee Hive, his escape from the Multnomah County jail, the time he'd served in Montana, and a few other petty crimes he'd been suspected of but never arrested for.

"The story is that he can slip through a transom window if it's cracked enough," the sergeant said. "If a fart could sneak through, so could this skinny kid."

Flemming spent the day phoning police departments and county jails: Tillamook, Salem, Portland, Tacoma, Seattle, even out in Pendleton, and The Dalles. She followed up with letters and telegraphs with a description of Layton: "Wanted in suspicion of the conflagration at the city of Astoria, Oregon. Consider him dangerous and apt to flee. Proceed with abundant speed and caution."

When she was done, she asked the desk sergeant to point her toward Frederick Blomquist, husband of the female dentist. Sure enough, Flemming found him that night on the far end of Commercial Street, a few blocks beyond the fire's reach, in a card room behind a bookstore. She stepped inside and motioned quickly with her badge. "Fire marshal. Frederick, a moment?" she called to a small room of five men around a table full of playing cards, ashtrays, and beer glasses.

A pudgy man stood up, calm and sure, and followed Flemming into the alley. He was middle-aged with graying hair and sags under his eyes. Flemming guessed a fifteen-year age difference with Asta. Frederick lit a cigarette.

"What's this about?" the dentist asked and then added, "ma'am."

"They take gold teeth in there for the ante?" Flemming smiled. "I imagine a man in your business might have a supply of those."

"Sadly no," Frederick retorted, "otherwise I'd be doing more to advertise for patients. Are you here to break up our game? Some kind of violation of the fire code?"

"I'm here to find out if you've seen Bart Layton. It seems your wife may have had an encounter with him the night of the fire."

"She told me," he said.

"And I wondered if, given this man's apparent interest in your wife, you've ever chanced upon him. Purposefully or not."

Frederick Blomquist drew a long drag from the cigarette and let it out slowly. "I'd love to. But for his sake, it'd probably be better if you ran into him first."

Flemming laughed a little. "Have a little manual dentistry you'd like to try out on him? You wouldn't be the first."

"Let's just say I'm a believer that people get what's coming to them," Frederick said. "I'm sorry I can't help you more than that. If there's nothing more . . ."

Flemming took a walk through the burned blocks of downtown Astoria. The gibbous moon cast a soft white light on what was left of the banks, restaurants, shops, and the theater. She stopped across the street from where the Bee Hive had been and retraced in her mind how the fire had spread, starting in the basement and tumbling in different directions like the arms of an octopus. Foster, the fire chief, had provided her with vivid details and a hand-drawn map. "Just hellish," he'd said helplessly.

It made sense that the fire, once ignited, produced the terrible damage that it did. The place was built to burn. She'd spent several days tracing the path of the fire, talking once again with the fire chief, and even examining the conditions of the fire hoses and pumper trucks that had been used. On the second day after her arrival the month before, she'd dug around the basement where it began, smelling the ashes in vain for anything that might have been an accelerant. *Kerosene, maybe?* It had burned too hot to leave behind much of an indication of how it'd started. There'd been a stove and plenty of coal and wood in storage. A single ignition point could've touched it off. *An accident? Possible but unlikely.*

As darkness fell Flemming was nearly to City Hall, at the far eastern edge of the burned area, when a hand grabbed her arm from behind. Reflexively she turned and swung her right elbow with force where an assailant's jaw might be. It found its mark with a glancing blow, and she heard a set of teeth clack together and then the low grunt of a man now on the ground. She was scared but didn't let on and instead stood over a small, older man checking for blood in his mouth.

"There's more of that if you'd like," she said, wondering if anyone else was nearby.

"No," came a small voice from the ground. "I would not like. I was only hoping to ask you a question. I'm Mr. Lukin. I own the laundry on Tenth."

"Mr. Lukin, I'm so sorry," Flemming said, squatting next to him with a handkerchief from her coat.

"No need for apologies. A woman has every obligation to self-defense," he said, still not convinced he wasn't bleeding. "You might consider a career in pugilism."

They stood up together, and Flemming brushed the dirt off his back. She realized she was talking to an old man, perhaps in his seventies, with a rail-thin body, hungry face, and eyes that seemed to struggle to remain contained in his head. She couldn't remember whether or not she'd met him in her interviews with the downtown merchants after the fire.

"My apologies again. Please, you had a question."

"Yes, I did. Can you tell me when you'll file your report? That's what I wanted to know. My insurance company is not going to proceed with my claim until your investigation has come to a close. A conclusion of some sort, that's apparently what they are in need of in order to—"

"I'm working as diligently as I can, Mr. Lukin, but these take time."

"Nothing gets rebuilt in my shop until your work is complete. Please, my family is running out of money. Do hurry."

Most insurance companies didn't rely on the completion of a fire investigator's report, but a few did when fraud was suspected or the fire was unusually costly. She considered it foot-dragging from insurers looking to hold on to every dollar before cutting a check, squeezing out any extra pennies of interest with every day of delay. Old Mr. Lukin produced a five-dollar bill from his pants pocket. "Can I help move things along?"

Flemming took the train back to Portland the next morning. Her sister Rachel was at their shared apartment when she got home, smoking and holding the lit cigarette out of the open, second-story window. A man Flemming didn't know was washing dishes in their sink wearing only pants and an undershirt. Rachel introduced him as Karl, one of the cooks at the café where she waited tables. Soon enough he disappeared without another word into Rachel's bedroom and shut the door behind him. Flemming raised an eyebrow at her sister.

"He's German. What can I say?" Rachel responded. "Not much for conversation."

"Don't suppose you had him here to discuss the classics."

"He wouldn't know one if it hit him between the teeth. How's the fire?"

"Strange. Still haven't put my arms around it, I'm afraid. Place of origin, I've got, right beneath one of the pool halls." Flemming started pacing the living room, lost in thought while her sister smoked. "No surprise that it moved so fast; they were never going to catch up to it. You should see this place, Rach. It's like they built a city on stilts made of match sticks. There are all these vents that just suck in air beneath every block, giving the fire everything it needed to jump in every direction. It's a goddamned mess."

"So it was started by . . . ?"

"Don't know. All sorts of loose threads." She explained the Finns and the Klan and the Chinese sauna and the dentist and the dentist's husband and this vanished man Layton. Karl reemerged from the bedroom, fully dressed now with his blond hair combed neatly to the side. He walked over to Rachel, gave her a kiss on the cheek, then sized up Flemming, noting her height.

"I have a friend, Ernst. I know he would love to meet with you. To spend time with you."

"Oh my, I'm flattered, Karl. I truly am," Flemming said, lilting her voice into its upper range. "Now if you would kindly consider taking this generous offer and stuffing it straight up—"

"Helen already has a suitor, I'm afraid," Rachel cut in. "Keeps her quite busy. But do tell your friend that she'll take a rain check, won't you?"

Karl's face showed confusion at the idiom, but he didn't pursue it further. When he was out the door, Flemming sent her thoughts straight back into Astoria. "What's baffling isn't that it burned, but why."

Flemming turned in the draft of her investigation report at the end of February 1923. Most of it was a recitation of where the fire started, how it spread, what techniques were used to combat it, and what damage had been caused. Just four sentences were dedicated to the cause: "It almost certainly was of incendiary origins. The true cause remains unclear as of this writing. Because of the explosive heat and the location of the fire's origin, we were unable to determine what kind of fuel may have been utilized. The investigation on the fire's origin remains an open inquiry."

Chapter 24

1923

The first letter that Asta Blomquist received from Bart Layton after the fire was postmarked in Tacoma, Washington. In mid-January 1923, about a month after the city burned down, one cream-colored sheet of paper in a small envelope arrived in her mailbox.

"Dearest, you know what I've done, but you mustn't tell anyone. A measure of who we are is the secrets we know to keep. Yours, B."

Another arrived the following week: a postcard of Mount Rainier.

"I have come to accept the news I received last year that you have married. I remain bewildered by it, but I wish you happiness. My 'big gesture' still stands and I hope that someday you'll see it as the sort of sign that means something to both of us."

And finally a third, some pencil scribblings on the back of a torn paper wrapper hastily stuffed into an envelope: "Two dentists in one family! How very strange that must be for you. Know that what I've done is done for the both of us. Yours for all time. B."

She'd kept them to herself, scared about what Frederick might say. He'd told his wife that the state marshal had visited with him about Bart, adding that "if that little sliver decides to visit, he might find out how hard it is to swim with a belt full of bricks around his waist." The last letter had crossed a line with her, though. The specificity of "two dentists" shook her out of the feeling that these notes could be safely disregarded if they were stuffed far enough into the back of her unmentionables drawer.

Asta gave all of the letters to H. H. Flemming the next time she was in Astoria. They met for coffee at Bly's Café near Uppertown. The fire investigator arrived first and enjoyed watching Asta come in the door, shake the mist off her hair, and dust it off her wool skirt. Flemming slowly read through the letters, smelled them, and read through them again.

"Horrible, isn't it?"

"It is." Flemming sighed. "A lovesick man is apt to do a lot of things. Start fires for one . . . They can also *claim* to start fires, use a natural opportunity to impress someone, take credit for something they didn't do. I've seen that a few times. Cowards are like that: people with something to prove but without the means or the will to actually prove it."

Asta stirred her coffee.

"Does this seem like something he would do?"

"To be honest I don't know him well enough to say one way or the other. And I'm not sure which is worse. Someone horrible enough to light the whole city on fire or someone who thinks I'd be impressed by that."

"We do a lot of things that don't make sense," Flemming said. "Especially a fellow like this who thinks his heart has been broken."

"It *wasn't*," Asta insisted, her voice rising. "I told you that. We barely ever spoke, and I certainly never sent him a signal that he and I would ever be an item. I'm married for God's sake, and about the last thing on my mind was some stranger I barely knew from back home."

"Well, he certainly felt like—"

"I think he's sick in the head, Inspector Flemming. I really do." Asta was exasperated now. "This isn't love, it's . . . it's some kind of disease that he can't get his mind right about this. I swear I never gave him any of these ideas."

Flemming gave her a broad smile. "Men are funny. He probably loved you anyway."

"He picked a hell of a way to show me, pardon my language. I don't appreciate it."

Flemming took the letters and made her way to Sheriff Slusher's office, spreading them out on his desk. She told the story that Asta Blomquist had recounted about the night of the fire and then what she'd said over coffee. Flemming explained that she'd spent days looking for Bart and had sent alerts to police stations on both sides of the river. Slusher shook his head in disbelief and fingered through a separate stack of papers and found what he was looking for.

"I got the damnedest thing right along these lines," Slusher said.

He showed Flemming the clipping from a newspaper ad from an astrologist named Celestrio in Buffalo, New York. Celestrio advertised "divinely inspired numerological and astrological services where futures are told, truths are revealed. Send one dollar, an exacting description of your personal situation, and birth dates for all involved. In six to eight weeks will come Celestrio's reply, illuminating relationships, foreseeing futures, and providing utmost tutoring to find the most enlightened path forward."

Flemming had seen the ad before in *The Morning Oregonian* and papers around the state. She shrugged at the sheriff, who then plucked another paper from his stack. It was a handwritten note that began "Dear Celestrio" and on the back was signed with the name Bart Layton. It was dated January 30, 1923, and the envelope had been postmarked from Seattle.

"Suppose that I have done something terrible but for all the right reasons," Bart began his letter. He went on to describe how he'd grown up with Asta but that their lives had separated, and she'd become a dentist and married another dentist, and how he'd been a thief who'd finally emerged from prison ready for normalcy and love. He mentioned the fire only at the end—"I'm sure you've read all about it in the papers"— and enclosed dates of birth for himself, Asta, and Frederick. The return address was a neighborhood in Seattle.

Celestrio had mailed a copy of Bart's letter to the Clatsop County Sheriff's Office in Astoria and included a note: "I can provide no relief to this young man. Perhaps you're a more proper recipient for this correspondence?"

Flemming read the letter twice and handed it back. "All told, sounds like we have our man. Perhaps it's time to take a trip to Seattle."

Slusher nodded. "Helluva way to win a woman back. Can't say I know one who'd be worth it, though."

That night Lem Becker stopped by the sheriff's house to talk through the particulars of an editorial he'd been considering for *The Western American*, an audacious piece designed to shore up support for consolidating all of the police powers—both city and county—under the sheriff's office. Becker was still shaking the rain off his coat in Slusher's living room when the sheriff began reciting the case of Bart Layton—the female dentist, the spurned affair, the letters, the confessions. All of it made Becker smile and forget the piece he'd planned to write.

"Outstanding. And I'll bet you good money," Becker said, "that this boy is as Red as they come."

Chapter 25

1923

A committee had been meeting in the basement of City Hall to map out ways to rebuild. There were arguments and shoving matches about which blocks would be fixed first, how the water and electricity lines would be run, and whether to start from the outside and move in or the other way around. The outgoing mayor and city council members were eventually wedged out of the meetings and the new Klan mayor and council members, with pushing and prodding from Lem Becker, put themselves in the lead.

Over the days and weeks after the fire, a plan emerged. Money and other pledges of support came in from Portland, Seattle, other cities in Oregon—even from Congress. The loss had been estimated at $15 million, and rebuilding the town would be something close to that. The incoming Klan city council employed a new city manager, a Klansman from La Grande, and began hiring dozens and dozens of people to remake the town. Determined not to repeat past mistakes, one of the first jobs—once the debris was cleared—would be to bring in hundreds of tons of sand dredged up from the Columbia's shipping channel and dump it into the giant hole beneath downtown.

Giffords was often in town to survey the progress and was pleased with what he saw. "Perhaps we hadn't intended to bite off quite this much, Mr. Becker, but it's better to have too big of an opportunity rather than too small," Giffords said. "The realm's work here, particularly in the aftermath of such an indelible crisis, will be remembered for a very long time."

There'd been rumors for a long time that the military wanted to build a new training camp for the Oregon National Guard, somewhere remote, with plenty of space to run around and shoot heavy artillery without the hassle of locals complaining about noise and early morning reveille. Astoria's city fathers had been after it for years. Thousands of soldiers at the camp would need somewhere to go on the weekend with dollars burning in every pocket. There was no space for a military camp in Astoria, of course. The city had been built on a hilly peninsula and was now pocked with houses. To the south, though, across Youngs Bay there were more than a hundred thousand acres of endless forest choked with fir, spruce, and a few herds of wandering elk.

Astoria's new mayor, a bug-eyed man named O. B. Setters, had barely been sworn in by late February 1923 when he led a few men from Fort Vancouver on a tour of the land. Setters had been swept into office with the other Klansman just before the fire, and he was eager to make his mark. Lem Becker had set the meeting up. Even though he didn't work for the mayor, Becker's marching orders from Atlanta had been to legitimize the Klan's leadership with the city, and this possible deal in the forest would go a long way toward that. They spent most of an afternoon tucked beneath umbrellas as they walked the property and discussed all manner of military drills, artillery exercises, barrack sizes, and even the possibility of clearing a strip for military planes to land. The state of Oregon already owned the land, so all that was needed was for the U.S. War Department to invest money into the training camp itself.

"There is a piece of history about this particular place you're standing on," Becker said near the end of their walkabout. He'd been quiet most of the time, making sure to let the new mayor appear to be in control of it all. "Less than a mile to the east, Lewis and Clark made their camp in the winter of 1805. Fort Clatsop, they called it. A miserable time, but they endured. Seems fitting that the U.S. military would return to train its bravest and finest. And if I might be a little presumptuous, I propose a name for our new joint endeavor: 'Camp Clatsop.'"

Setters, who'd known nothing about the idea, spoke up to mumble, "Yes, something we've been considering for some time."

They walked a bit longer and stopped in a clearing where wet ferns gathered around their knees and the rain poured over their umbrellas.

"I'm troubled by something," said one of the military men, a Lieutenant Deeks. "There seems to be a Red streak here a mile wide and a mile deep. They've run amok is how I hear it. I don't see how we justify a military exercise operation in the heart of so much socialism or communism or whatever 'ism' you might call it that isn't genuine red, white, and blue. Do you follow?"

"Well . . ." Setters began without any sense of where he was going.

The lieutenant interrupted and saved him the discomfort. "War efforts are directly controlled by Congress, and I've got committee members looking square up my back entrance on every manner of decision when it comes to spending on these training camps. Can I in good conscience tell him this isn't a hotbed of forces in direct contravention of our country's interest?"

"It'd be hard to deny that there hasn't been a history—" Becker started.

Deeks cut him off. "I'm not talking about history here." His voice tightened with anger. "The goddamned Reds burned your entire city to the ground a few weeks ago! And the best I can tell, not a single man has been arrested, detained, or even taken out to the woodshed over this. Do I have that about right?"

Setters cleared a frog from his throat and spoke, "There has certainly been evidence—strong evidence—that these sympathizers had a role in the fire."

"To hell with *evidence*," Deeks said. "That has nothing to do with this. What I know, and what members of the committee will know, is that this is the place where radicals burn entire city blocks with little more than disapproval from the city fathers. That's going to be a very goddamn hard sell to them, and it's not a risk I'm going to take until this situation has been sufficiently handled. It's a deal-breaker, gentlemen. Fix it, and maybe we can talk."

With that, they all walked back to their cars. The military men drove south, and Becker and Setters drove north toward Astoria, the ride silent except for Becker vowing, "This will be taken care of."

A few nights later five men from the city found Brewster, the Wobblies' itinerant recruiter, in a one-bedroom cabin he'd been renting in the woods at Tongue Point, just east of Astoria. Their faces were covered by handkerchiefs, and two of them held blocks of wood.

"Ready for this, are we boys?" Brewster said after he assessed the small mob at his door and then laughed a little. "Is this all they could round up for this job?"

"This is going to be plenty," one of them growled and took a step forward.

With a single motion Brewster swept his hand across the top of the doorjamb and found a small pistol he kept for emergencies. He fired two quick shots, one tearing a wad of flesh from the shoulder of the closest man, sending him to the ground in a howling heap. The rest of the men descended on Brewster, slapping the gun from his hand and pummeling his body with kicks and punches. Brewster had spent a lifetime brawling and knew how to get his licks in by slashing his elbows at eyebrows and thrusting knees into groins.

"You little girls," he called out.

There was a long minute of chaos in the doorway of the house as a mass of grunting bodies swarmed against each other in violence. Finally the man who'd been shot brought a piece of wood down onto Brewster's forehead, unleashing a torrent of blood across his face. The blow stunned Brewster long enough for the other men to bunch his arms behind him and thrust him into a chair inside the house.

One of the men gathered Brewster's hair into his hands and thrust his head up.

"I think we've had just enough of you and your Red friends," the man said calmly.

Brewster's vision was fuzzy. He struggled to blink away the blood flowing into his eyes. "I'm sure . . . the feeling . . . is mutual."

Just then one of the men holding one of Brewster's arms jerked it high and forced a sickening pop from his shoulder. Brewster screamed, and a closed fist knocked out one of his teeth. He spat it into the chest of one of the men, who caught it and examined it in the light of a lamp.

"Partial payment in restitution," the man said. "Not paid in full, but it's a start. We'll be back later to collect the rest."

Sure enough the handful of men—minus the one who had been shot—returned early the next morning, just as the sun was fighting its way through the gauze of the marine layer. They didn't bother to knock and found Brewster asleep on his couch, the blood on his shirt and pants now a layer of brown cake. Someone slapped his boots to wake him up. Brewster groaned, and his eyes adjusted to the dark figures surrounding him in his half-dream state. He recognized them as they stood in a semicircle around the sofa, noticing a bulky man at one end whose head was squeezed into a cowboy hat a size or two too small. Brewster discerned that the man was Sheriff Slusher. They'd run into each other last fall when the lawman found him passing out handbills outside a speakeasy near Warrenton. Slusher had a deputy drive him clear out past Knappa and drop him in the Brownsville slough.

"I'd offer you fellows some coffee if I thought . . ."

Something else hit the bottom of his boots, a stick of some sort.

"Hey, haven't we already—"

"We have and there's no reason to go through that again, Mr. Brewster." It was Slusher talking, but Brewster tried to remember if he'd seen him the night before. "Of course, we'd be happy to finish our little dentistry project, if you'd care to."

Brewster gathered himself and sat up on the sofa, feeling the fleshy gap in his gums where his tooth had been and wincing at white-hot rods of pain in his head and shoulder. These men weren't professionals, but they knew their way around the brutality game. Someone handed him a single piece of paper, a typed affidavit with his name at the top and a few paragraphs beneath that Brewster tried to skim but found his eyes protesting. There were references to the great fire in Astoria a few months back, incitement of revolution, and a conversation with a man he'd never heard of, someone called Layton. A pen was thrust into his hand.

"Your signature is all that's needed, Mr. Brewster," Slusher said, low and calm. "Unless you'd rather part with the rest of your teeth. I'll leave that choice to you, but I would advise you to think carefully before you decide."

Brewster let a long moment pass. The remnants of his broken furniture were scattered across the small cabin, and the faces of the men featured a kind of cruel indifference that he'd seen in union busters, crooked policemen, the old Pinkertons, hired thugs, and anyone else paid to drain the humanity from existence in exchange for expediency and profit. *Why are there always more of these mouth-breathing bastards than us?*

Brewster, tired and bloody, signed without fully grasping the words on the page. As soon as it was done, one man snatched the pen from his hand and another punched him across the jaw with a fist that felt like a hammer. "Be gone by noon and never come back."

Chapter 26

1923

Sheriff Slusher and H. H. Flemming didn't find Bart Layton at the address given in the letter to the astrologer. In fact there was no building that even matched that number. It was Slusher's idea to check with the Seattle police. Sure enough, Layton was being held in the city jail for shoplifting two pairs of women's shoes. They had an hour to kill before they could meet with Layton, so Flemming took them to a speakeasy she knew near Queen Anne Hill. Flemming had a beer, but Slusher refused with a wave of his hand.

"Whatever do you get by keeping company with Lem Becker and these men in the not-so-invisible empire?" Flemming said, leaning forward. "Explain that allure to me."

Slusher shrugged. "There isn't much to explain. We live in evil times, and good will never win if men act alone. They need to be part of something."

Flemming laughed, took a big draw from her mug, and let the first airy threads of intoxication wash into her brain. "And this is winning? How many skulls have you cracked with that sap of yours?"

"Enough," Slusher said. "At least enough to get the notice of some very important people. My name's been put in for the state prison warden's job."

"Well, maybe you whack a few more people and find your way into the governor's mansion in Salem."

Slusher let out his own small laugh. "Maybe so."

The jail was a brick building that smelled like grease and leaking pipes. Flemming had managed to down two beers and was glad of it when they were deep inside the building's winding halls and windowless walls.

Layton was thin with dark curly hair and a slightly hunted look. "I am not the man you seek," he said wearily before he was even let out of his cell.

Flemming smiled at him through the bars. "I think you might be."

"Who the hell are you?" Layton asked Flemming.

"I'm the someone left to clean up your mess from last year."

The three were escorted by a sergeant into a brick interrogation room down the hall. Slusher sat quietly and watched Flemming methodically fan out the letters from Asta on the table. Layton watched too, lacing his fingers together on top of the table with half a smile.

"Mr. Layton, we're here because of the fire. I think you know the one," Flemming started.

"Uh, San Francisco, right? After the earthquake?"

Flemming didn't laugh but Slusher started to and then caught himself.

"Mr. Layton, people died in the Astoria fire. Are you aware of that?" Flemming leaned in. "Did you write these letters?"

Bart kept his hands locked together but craned his neck to let his sleepy eyes scan the papers.

"Handwriting's familiar," he said. "That's about all I can say."

Flemming read each letter aloud, starting with the date and ending with each sign-off. There was no need for any sort of dramatic rendition. Then she read the letter to Celestrio, the astrologer, and locked eyes with Bart across the table. "You wrote those, right?"

Bart didn't move, so Flemming pressed on. "So you thought Miss Blomquist was going to be your girl, but the universe had another idea, so you decided to burn the whole place down. Is that about right?"

Flemming let out a long breath and lowered her voice so much that Slusher had to turn an ear toward her. "Heartbreak is a steep hill to climb by yourself. Trust me, I know that well. It's a black, black place that seems to have no beginning and no end and is just, just . . . Sometimes we lash out and we hope it takes the pain away, or at least sends it along to someone else, if even for a moment."

Bart stipulated that possibility with a small, thoughtful pucker of his lips. She met his eyes. "Is that why you did it? Were you just tired and you lashed out?"

"I am tired, ma'am. I've been tired for a long time."

Slusher cleared his throat and pulled a piece of paper from his coat. "We know the other reason you started this fire. I, for one, find this the most sickening."

He let Bart read the affidavit from Brewster and then pulled out the choicest excerpt to read aloud. "Maybe this sounds familiar: 'Mr. Layton and I shared a political affiliation and affinity for revolution. In fact he was an avid reader and distributor of our pamphlets. He talked of starting a fire in the name of the Red cause, and I guess that's what he ultimately did.'"

Bart's eyes widened and he shook his head in disbelief. "That's a lie!"

"That's the sworn statement of one of the most notorious Wobbly organizers ever to come to Oregon. And as far as I know he's got no reason to lie," Slusher said. "Why don't you just tell us what happened?"

Flemming had known about the letter and had suspected it'd been concocted under duress, possibly altogether fictionalized, but had no way of knowing and no choice but to let Slusher play that card. Emotion welled up in Bart, first anger and then tears that rimmed his eyelids. He buried his head in his arms like a child. "What kind of fix is this?"

Flemming let the young man sob quietly and then cracked a sly smile to shift the mood. "Do you know the postmaster back in Knappton has some strong feelings about you? Seems someone stole his father's glasses some time ago and the poor old fellow stepped off the dock and drowned."

Bart didn't say anything.

"Did you take those glasses?"

Bart lifted his head and nodded. "I did. I meant no harm."

"I know," Flemming responded. "But Bart we're here today because we need to resolve this issue in Astoria. Can you help us or not?"

Another long silence set in, and Flemming tried not to break her focus from Bart, knowing they'd arrived at a moment to do or die. Finally Bart unlaced his fingers and pushed all the letters back toward Flemming.

"I'm not the man you're looking for," Bart said quietly. "I'm sorry."

Flemming raised her voice. "Now look," she said. "We've got dead people and an entire city in ruins—"

"I said I'm sorry, and I meant it."

They didn't have a confession from Bart Layton, but they arrested him anyway. The letters and Asta and Brewster would be enough.

At the trial in November 1923 Flemming was called to the Clatsop County Courthouse to testify about the fire, the damage, the origins, and her ultimate conclusion that Bart Layton had been the arsonist. Bart's letters to Asta Blomquist were read into the record, and his attorney—a rumpled man who seemed only half-interested in the proceedings—asked just a few questions during cross-examination. Oddly, he was most interested in the letter from Bart to Celestrio, the astrologist in Buffalo. He spent several long minutes attempting to impugn the efficacy of astrology. "There is simply no predictive qualities in the stars, none whatsoever," he said during his most heated moment. Bart rose briefly—to the disbelief of his own attorney—to begin a rebuttal, but the judge cut him off with a jagged swipe of his finger.

The trial took two days, and Bart was found guilty of two counts of first-degree arson. He protested but only slightly. "The fix is in, that much is obvious," Bart said on the stand, searching in vain for Asta in the gallery. "What's done is done, and whatever I done, I done for love."

Flemming was in Estacada, east of Portland, investigating a hotel fire that had incinerated two men on a hunting trip when she read the news in the morning paper. Ten years in the Oregon State Penitentiary for Bart Layton. She set down her coffee and let out a long breath.

Chapter 27

1924

Lem Becker was never promoted, and the Ku Klux Klan never offered him a new job. Astoria became consumed with rebuilding itself, and, even though the Klan's men ran the city government, no one cared that they had led the way. It was a sour victory made worse by the fact that the Klan itself was imploding, at least in Oregon. Rumors had circulated for years that Fred Giffords had been skimming money and funneling it to a new car and a house on the coast of California. But finally this gossip gained traction and made it into the newspapers along with some incriminating minutes of Klan meetings around the state. Becker, some said, had made sure of that. Giffords attempted a feeble defense in the papers, something about accounting errors, but ultimately left town the night before he was supposed to meet some of the men from Atlanta.

But the rank and file members turned on Becker, too, since the two men had been linked together for so long. The offices of *The Western American* were ransacked during a storm in December 1924. Many of Becker's supplies were stolen or wrecked, and fetid bits of rotten salmon were scattered from wall to wall. All the windows were shattered, and the legs were sawed off his desk chair. A salmon's head anchored a note on his desk: "Your Americanism is for shit."

Becker called the police station and told Leb Karlsson, the chief, about the burglary. Several hours later H. H. Flemming showed up and found Becker tidying up, holding a towel across his face to block the stench of the fish.

"What are you doing here?" Becker asked her. "There's no fire."

She'd been just a few miles away, down in Gearhart looking into a fire at a car lot, when she got word from Karlsson about the break-in.

"It's always a shame when bad things happen to good people," Flemming said, unbothered by the smell as she surveyed the damage. "That's not the case in this particular instance, but it's a shame when it happens."

"It doesn't bother you that a proprietor's business has been vandalized?"

Flemming pulled a matchbox from her coat pocket, struck a match, and threw it in the trash bin next to the desk. Becker scrambled to put it out, stamping the small flames erupting on the edges of the paper. Flemming threw another lit match on top of the desk and launched a third as she strolled across the room.

"What bothers me," Flemming said, patting her pockets in search of another box of matches, "is that you seem so bothered by the thought of a fire in this little shithole of an office."

She found what she was looking for and began striking one match after another, tossing them over her shoulder and across the room and into the piles of aging newspapers stacked by the door. Becker pounced at each one, stomping on the flames and smothering them with his coat. A few fist-sized fires still managed to break out here and there, the smoke mixing with the fish odor.

"This is nonsense! Will you stop that?"

The fire investigator paused to let another thought set in. "I will . . . not," she said, holding an unlit match. "I've been hearing troubling things about you, Mr. Becker. Do you have any sense of what the fire cost?"

"Which fire?"

Flemming advanced on him quickly and slammed him against the wall. Becker was taken aback by her animal strength. "You know goddamned well which fire," she spit out.

Becker blinked hard as Flemming put her weight against the man's chest.

"Millions—I know it was millions of dollars," he said finally.

"Not the money. Who gives a shit about the money? You think I care about the money?" Flemming backed off and resumed tossing lit matches around the room. Becker stopped trying to put them out.

"Two people died and one man went to prison," she said finally, lowering her voice. "And I know for a fact that you and your band of hooded meatheads were the responsible parties. And if you're responsible for the fire, you're responsible for the deaths of two people and that, in my book, is murder."

Becker straightened himself and squared his shoulders at Flemming with a broad smile. "Well, that surprises me a great deal, Inspector Flemming, because I seem to recall you testifying at the trial of a young man who'd been convicted of that crime. Cased closed, is it not?"

Ever since Bart Layton was sent to prison, rumors had found their way to Flemming, whispers that Becker and his Klansmen had set the fire that destroyed Astoria. The motive varied; some stories said the blaze was lit out of revenge against the Bee Hive's stubborn owners after their reluctance to join the Klan. Others assigned broader political purposes or said Becker himself had started it as part of a complex insurance scheme in conjunction with a few of the downtown building owners. Flemming had returned to chase each new iteration only to find it dissipate like the thick layer of marine air over Astoria that arrived and departed at whim. She lost sleep, drank more, and had a pit in her stomach that never seemed to fade.

"It's only a matter of time before someone turns on you, and then it's going to be your ass locked away for this," Flemming seethed.

"That would be a pity," Becker said, pretending to ponder the idea of prison. "I don't suppose a man like me would fare very well in a den of deviants like that. The good news, Inspector Flemming, is that prospect hinges on some mighty speculative elements that seem unlikely to bear fruit, especially since our fair town is plenty pleased to have someone already arrested and convicted for this terrible crime and rotting in a jail cell."

Flemming grabbed Becker's head with one hand and slammed it violently onto the desk, then used her other hand to smother his face with the salmon head. White juice sluiced from its gills and open mouth into a puddle beneath his chin. Becker shut his eyes tight, feeling the room spinning violently around him.

She spoke low into his ear. "If you're not out of this city by the first light tomorrow, I'm going to find you, split your balls with a number fourteen hook, and drag you out to the spit with ten-pound weights in your pockets."

Part 6 *Ashes*

Chapter 28

1922

By Lem Becker's thinking, the fire was intended to serve a simple purpose: Put a quick but dramatic scare into the town and allow the Klan's newly elected candidates—men who stood on unsure footing with the community—to sweep in and save the day. Then allow a block or two of the city to burn and have it rebuilt by the new mayor, the first step in reimagining the town into a great port city worthy of its perfect location and new sense of morality, ingenuity, and economic prosperity. "HQ in Atlanta knows the value of seismic events," Fred Giffords had told him. "Progress needn't always be incremental."

During his time in Astoria, Becker couldn't help but notice that Mr. Anderson, who'd owned the Bee Hive for years, had rebuffed every subtle attempt to recruit him into the Klan. He wasn't a Catholic or a Jew or a foreigner, so it always grated on Becker that this man at the heart of downtown should spurn membership in the city's most important movement.

"We provide goods for all here, Mr. Becker," Anderson had said once. "I make no exception for religion or nationality, and neither will the Bee Hive. Once you take that road, I suspect, you find that everything becomes divisible by two and eventually you find yourself standing alone in a city full of other people standing alone. And that's not a city."

December 8, 1922, was a Catholic holy day, the Feast of the Immaculate Conception. "There's a little poetry here, don't you think?" Becker had suggested to John G. Smith before things turned sour at the Youngs River.

Smith did as he was instructed. He went into town the evening before and found a boarding house near the river to spend the night. It was cheap and drafty, but it would do. He'd had a knot of acid in his stomach since their meeting, certain that he'd go through with it but equally certain that odds were against it turning out as well as Becker said it would. "Shoot a bear in the ass and don't expect to enjoy the result," his grandfather had liked to say.

Stopping on Bond Street, Smith swallowed two drinks in a backroom and spent the next several hours on the docks in a grim wait. The river was still except for the bar pilots in their small, motorized boats making their way out to the ships to escort them across the treacherous sand bar between the river and the ocean. *How many men have died in the bedlam at the end of the Columbia, just like my father's friend Jorma? The world claims what it will whenever it likes. There is no reason for it*, he figured. *Die in the chaos of the river or asleep in your bed. The ultimate consequence is the same.*

As Becker said there would be, he found an unlocked door and a small passageway beneath the pool hall that connected to the basement cavern under the Bee Hive. And, again as Becker promised, there were bags of coal and stacks of wood to feed the massive furnace in the middle of the room. He took his time carefully carrying out Becker's instructions, first creating two large piles of wood and coal against the east and west walls, which were made of thick beams of stacked Douglas fir. From the furnace he laid two lines of thinner bits of firewood and coal to carry the flame to the outside of the room where the piles were. Finally, from a small tin of kerosene that he'd brought from Olney—stolen from the maintenance shed and stashed in the inner pocket of his coat—he doused the large piles first and then the feeder lines leading to the middle of the room, stopping about three feet from the furnace.

Smith sat for some time on a wooden chair in front of the giant furnace, listening as the fire churned inside like a satisfied beast eating its fill. Waves of heat pulsed across his face. *Walk away now and no crime's been committed*, he thought. *Setting the stage for disaster is not yet disaster.*

He wondered why he'd never married and noted that Lily hadn't either. Neither would bear children, he suspected. The line of the Leino family would end here, in Astoria, so far from home. Maybe. Or maybe he would do this deed tonight and Lily would find her way back to Finland, and maybe their aunt and uncle's farm waited for her, and maybe there was a husband who waited too, and children to be born, and meals to be shared around a crowded, happy dinner table during those beautiful yet painfully cold winter nights that seemed to last an eternity. Maybe.

He smiled to himself, poured the last line of kerosene connecting the feeder lines and furnace, lit the match, and went out the same way he came in.

The street was mostly quiet, and Smith ran around to the back of the block to make sure his work took hold. Soon enough he saw an orange glow shimmering from a basement window as little flecks of snow and rain began to fall on his face. Nothing to be undone now. Within minutes the fire was hissing and crackling as it ate into the wood and the bags of coal. There were shouts of surprise, first from a single person and then many. Flames were visible now from the street, and somewhere an alarm bell rang and rang and rang into the frigid night.

Suddenly a door swung up at the top of the back stairs and a man appeared. Smoke roiled from the opening as he picked his way down toward the street, clattering over the wooden steps, nearly tumbling sideways over the wobbly railing. *Is there someone in the Bee Hive in the middle of the night?*

The man was out of breath by the time he reached Smith, and his dark, curly hair and face were slick with the sweat of panic and exertion.

"What's happened?"

"A fire," Smith replied flatly, exchanging a glance with the stranger. They watched together for a long minute, marveling at the fire's speed as it ate into the building's walls and flirted with the adjacent ones.

"My God," the man said. "It's incredible. Almost beautiful."

The man gathered his coat around himself and then jumped a little—as if he'd been startled—and sprinted toward Commercial Street. Smith took two big steps back into the shadows and sighed as the city began to burn.

With the heat at his back, Smith walked quickly to the Sanborn docks at the bottom of Eighth Street to meet Becker, as arranged, and collect the rest of his payment. Instead he found three men he'd never seen before, all of them in long wool coats and hats pulled down. Two of them grabbed his arms and the other put a cold, wet rope around his neck. Its rough fibers jabbed his skin and then it tightened. Confused, he panicked and fought back but found burly arms holding him stiff.

The men were from the klavern down in Medford, loyalists who knew the importance of adhering to the code. Becker had liked what they'd done in Jacksonville, Oregon, earlier that year with a few businessmen who were bucking their efforts: A grocer, a wood-seller, and an electrician were snatched from their homes, blindfolded, and taken into the Rogue forest where a rope was laced around each of their necks and over the branch of a tree. Two of the Klansmen pulled the ropes hard enough to lift the businessmen off the ground, everything but the tips of their toes. Becker imagined the awkward and macabre dance this induced, each man hovering over his own grave while stretching his toes the farthest they could stretch in pursuit of breath. They called it a necktie hanging, and after a few terrifying moments, the men were released with a stern warning and enough of a scare to join the Klan's ranks the next day.

Becker had ordered the same procedure for Smith, to coincide with a warning: Take your money and keep your mouth shut. "We'll keep our end of the bargain," Becker had instructed his men, "but he needs to do his part. He needs to know we mean forever."

The men looped the rope around the boards on the Sanborn dock and pulled, lifting Smith off his feet until only his shoe tips touched. He kicked once, twice, and finally one of the river rocks that provided him the tiniest relief rolled toward the river. It was dark and noisy and still chaotic as the fire burned behind them, and no one saw that Smith had lost anything to stand on. One of the men punched him in the stomach and Smith felt a warm darkness start to fill his head and eyes.

"Snitches get the worst end of the rope," someone hissed in his ear. "Remember that if you start thinking about changing your mind about our agreement."

Smith found one last reservoir of primal energy and clawed between the rope and his neck to create an avenue of air into his windpipe. Someone slapped his hand away. For a moment in his mind, he saw the sun stealing its way into the dark forest in Olney, golden rays painting every leaf and tree trunk in brilliant color. Even the stumps looked to be alive again. The world was radiant and good and ready for something better, if only for a fleeting second. Arni Leino's mouth edged toward a smile—was John G. Smith smiling too?—but the spell was broken by the last words in his ear, heavy with the smell of whiskey, "If you ever . . ."

Chapter 29

1923

No one came to John G. Smith's funeral. The newspapers had mentioned him just once amid the chaos of the coverage of the fire—a suicide by hanging, they insisted—and his body was placed in a pine box and lowered into a shallow hole at Greenville Cemetery on the hill above town, within sight of the Columbia's mouth. It was a dark Monday in mid-January 1923, and the seagulls were riding whatever thin wisps of cool air had ridden east across the ocean and been welcomed on the Pacific coast.

E. B. Harrington, the coroner, was unhappy that the job of eulogizing this stranger, who apparently had no friends and no family to speak of, had fallen to him. Before the first shovelfuls of dirt were tossed onto the box, Harrington raised his hand and his two helpers paused, letting their wool coats dance in the salty breeze while they leaned on their shovel handles.

"Passing through this world, it's never an easy thing. We walk many roads," Harrington began, unsure of where his impromptu sermon was leading him. "We find ourselves lost on most occasions. And oddly enough we become lost in the places most familiar to us: the well-trodden paths, the hallway between rooms, the fleeting moment between drawing our first breath and exhaling our last. It doesn't last long, does it? And it's a pity we spend so much of it alone and wondering if we will always be alone."

The grave diggers set down their shovels but stopped listening, choosing instead to look at some far, unseen object somewhere toward the ocean. Harrington shrugged and supposed his talk had taken a darker turn than he'd anticipated.

"But there is sunshine too," he continued. "It does not come on all days. We of all people know that. But when it does, we should be grateful. And maybe, if we're lucky, our final reward is one more endless day in the gaze of the sun." Harrington paused again. "Farewell then, stranger, and safe journey."

There was no grave marker. As the men filled the hole, Harrington made careful note of the grave's location on a map in his leather ledger and, seeing that rain threatened, made his way back to town.

Lily didn't find out about her brother until a week after the fire when someone left an old newspaper in her cell. The story was only three paragraphs, buried at the bottom of a single column on the bottom of the front page. She wept and wept until she vomited from the heartache. The guards at the jail thought she had lost her mind.

Months later, as the first signs of spring laid in, Lily's cell door opened and the guard stepped aside, beckoning her to leave. Confused, she waited several beats and then walked out. A tall, gaunt man she didn't know met her outside the jail's entrance with an envelope and a message: "Your brother has secured your safe passage home, and I highly recommend you take it without delay."

He held the envelope in front of her, but she made no movement toward it.

Epilogue

1947

In the spring of 1947 H. H. Flemming spent two days driving, first north and then east, to get to Medical Lake, not far from Spokane, Washington. The only thing there, really, was Eastern State Hospital, a warren of block-shaped brick buildings tucked innocuously in the pines amid an expanse of wide, rolling hills.

The visiting room was beige and empty except for a metal table, two metal chairs, and a small window up high on one wall, where a few streaks of dull daylight snuck in. The man was already at the table when she arrived. Except for the dark eyes, he really looked nothing like the man Flemming and Slusher had first interviewed so long ago in the Seattle jail. The man's hair, once dark and curly, was now sparse and mostly gray. His body had grown thick and soft, his face sagged, and there were green bruises around his eyes.

"New therapy," Bart Layton said, trying to coax a smile from himself. "It's pretty terrible."

"I heard they were doing that now," Flemming said, trying not to stare. "How you doing, Bart? Do you remember me?"

"Seems like more of us get the shock than don't in here."

They looked for a long moment across the table at one another.

"I don't remember, no."

Flemming reintroduced herself and reminded him of the fire and Asta Blomquist and his arrest in Seattle and the trial in Astoria. Bart had done his time in the Oregon State Penitentiary and then moved to California, where he'd become a thief again and spent another half-dozen years in Folsom. He was married for a time, took a job as a deckhand on a crab boat in Alaska, and was arrested again in Seattle after stealing a boat from a marina on the eastern reaches of the Puget Sound. He'd been sure the boat had belonged to a woman he'd once loved. The judge had sent him to Eastern State outside of Spokane in the hopes of a "medically induced mental treatment for habitual criminal behavior and persistent aberrant thoughts." Bart had escaped the hospital once, partnering with a string bean of a man who swore he was president and was urgently needed in Washington, D.C. Before they could part ways, they were caught by a farmer and his son who'd read about the escapees in the paper and were stunned to find them sharing a cigarette at the edge of their wheat field, docile as lambs.

Flemming was now in her final year with the state fire marshal's office. She'd worked hundreds of fires since Astoria, and all of it was a blur of blackened destruction, death, lies, scams, and the faces of those she'd sent to prison or quietly let off based on her own internal code of who deserved punishment and who didn't. The Astoria fire still nagged, though. Bart Layton had served his time and moved on to the rest of his fractured life, but she hadn't quite closed the book. Rachel moved out a few years after Astoria; she married a traveling furniture salesman, settled in Minnesota, and produced a family of her own. Flemming had two unlikely flirtations with love, one with a man and another with a woman, but never arrived at anywhere permanent. She kept working, kept writing reports, her hand beginning to cripple with arthritis in the grip of government pens.

Astoria, too, had found its way. The city rebuilt and the fire seemed to dispel some of the demons that had taken root. After the end of prohibition, beer flowed freely, respectable businesses opened on Taylor and Bond streets, and the gangs moved along. Even the Klan finally wandered off. Lem Becker left Astoria shortly after the break-in at *The Western American* and turned up dead, stabbed through the lung from behind on a logging road near Mount Hood in the fall of 1925.

And here was Bart Layton, this damaged outline of a soul hovering like a ghost among the smell of industrial bleach and stale pee.

Flemming recounted for him what had happened in 1922. Bart barely looked at the fire marshal, and finally a few of the details slowly began to seep through the fog, though they played through his mind like a dream from long ago, and he was unsure what exactly was real and what had been conjured from a counterfeit world. Some things he was sure of, though.

"I didn't start that fire," Bart said when Flemming was finally done speaking, rubbing eyes that were red with exhaustion. "I didn't, and I wouldn't. I broke into the Bee Hive, I chased after Asta best as I could—I'm not ashamed of that; she was a great gal—but I'm no firebug."

"I know."

The two stared at each other, and the day's weight settled in.

"How's the food in here?" Flemming eventually offered.

Bart didn't seem to hear her question at first so it lingered, and Flemming became lost in considering the administration of pain that this hollowed man had endured in this institution. Electroshock therapy wasn't discussed much in public, but it was known enough for someone like Flemming to understand. She wondered how many volts it took to rearrange a man's being and considered the fickleness of both human and machine. One tweak of the knob too far and . . .

"It's the worst," Bart finally said, smiling with a bit of clarity on his face. "The absolute worst. But I eat it. We all do because that's what's put on our plate. What choice do we have?"

Now it was Flemming's turn to let the question sit on the air, unanswered. After a few moments, a muscular orderly in white pants and a white T-shirt opened the door and clicked at Bart in the same way one would call a horse.

"Time to saddle up," the orderly said in a low voice. "Hi-ho."

Flemming reached across the table to touch Bart's hand, but he was on his feet before their fingers met. As he walked toward the orderly, a man shouted in the hallway, a long indecipherable plea of some kind. And then, in an instant, Bart Layton was out the door and gone.

9 781496 235220